BLURB

Joe Wilder has never had a long-term romantic relationship. He's a cheater, a rogue, a flirt, a womanizer. He ruins everything.

Until he meets Sadie.

They fall into an unorthodox friendship, meeting once a month on a park bench to share a lunch and stories of Joe's sexual conquests, but soon Joe discovers that once a month is not enough. Relentless bachelorhood is not enough. All those women…not enough.

Yet Sadie has troubles of her own, and no matter what Joe wants, he can't make himself what she needs. It will take personal tragedy for both of them to find their way to each other, but can a love that grew from such rocky soil ever be expected to bloom?

Or will he once again ruin it all, and leave it not only broken, but shattered?

Shattered is a companion novella to Broken. The story features new material as well as scenes from Broken retold in Joe's point of view. Readers who have not read Broken may want to read it, first.

SHATTERED

MEGAN HART

Shattered
Megan Hart
Chaos Publishing

Copyright© 2020 Megan Hart
Chaos Edition, License Notes

All rights reserved.

No part of this book may be reproduced in any form or by any electronic or mechanical means, including information storage and retrieval systems, without written permission from the author, except for the use of brief quotations in a book review.

ebook ISBN: 978-1-951868-04-8
print ISBN: 978-1-951868-05-5

photo credit:MaRoPictures
cover: Chaos

ALSO BY MEGAN HART

All Fall Down

All the Lies We Tell

All the Secrets We Keep

A Heart Full of Stars

Always You

Broken

Beg For It

By the Sea of Sand

Castle in the Sand

Clearwater

Dirty

Hold Me Close

Hurt the One You Love

Naked

Passion Model

Precious and Fragile Things

Ride with the Devil

Stumble into Love

The Favor

The Resurrected One: First Come the Storms

Womb

Unforgivable

Pleasure and Purpose

No Greater Pleasure

Selfish Is the Heart

Virtue and Vice

Beautiful Thorns

ONE

January

There was a woman sitting on Joe's bench.

He'd been bringing his lunch here to the atrium in cool weather, or to the garden outside in warmer, for a little over six months. It was a nice place, a private place, and usually empty. Until today.

"Hi," the woman said after a long moment in which he'd only stared with his takeout bag from the *Yes, Ma'am Sub Shop* clutched in one fist and his overlarge travel mug of coffee in the other. "Am I in your spot? I can move, if you want —"

"This is the only good bench," Joe said. "The other one has splinters, and birds leave a mess on it."

More silence. She stared up at him with an open expression. Blue eyes. Sandy blond hair. She was pretty, but weren't they all? No, Joe thought after a second, surprised at himself. She was pretty the way only she was.

On her lap she balanced a glass container of salad, and next to her on the bench lay a cloth napkin with half a baguette on it. The bread had a bite taken out of it, and he found himself fascinated, for a moment, about the shape her teeth had left behind.

"There's plenty of room," the woman said. "I can move over."

"If you don't mind." Joe watched her eyes for that familiar glimmer. That spark of interest, the slow quirk of a smile, maybe even the slide of her tongue over her lower lip.

An invitation.

Women usually looked at him that way. Like he was an item on the menu, and they were very, very hungry. Not every woman, of course. Just most of them.

This woman, however, merely scooted over, lifting her baguette and settling it into the bowl of salad while she tucked the napkin onto her lap. She smiled at Joe, sure, but the curve of her lips was neutral and not assessing. Not covetous. It was the smile she probably would have given any stranger.

He sat.

"Thank you," he said.

"No problem at all." Her voice rasped. Not like she had a cold. More like she'd been crying. There was no sign of redness or tears in her eyes, yet everything about her seemed bent beneath the heaviness of grief.

The bench was wide enough for both of them to sit without touching one another. Joe set his cup on the bench's arm so he could pull out his sandwich and the small bag of chips, along with a handful of napkins. He pressed the paper bag onto his knees and put the food on top of it, very aware of the clink of her fork against the glass and the subtle brushing noise she made when she wiped her lips with the cloth napkin.

He glanced at her. "Fancy."

Her laugh took a few seconds to show up, but the wait was worth it. Low and bubbling with a hint of surprise, her chuckle warmed him. If she *had* been crying, he thought, maybe she'd feel a little better, now.

"I guess so. I guess I think of cloth napkins as a way of treating myself to something nice. I'm not likely to go out to a nice restaurant every day for lunch, but I can make my own nice experience for myself." She twisted a bit on the bench to half face him and looked down at his lunch. "I've never ordered from *Yes, Ma'am*. I hear they're good."

He unwrapped the sandwich and lifted the top bun to reveal the sliced tomatoes he'd specifically ordered be left off. "When they get the order right, it's pretty good. I hate tomatoes."

"You could take it back," she suggested.

Joe shook his head. "Too hungry now. Besides, if I complain, the owner will spank the guy who made the sandwich, and I can't have that on my conscience."

"Spank...Oh, right." She laughed again and gave a little wave toward the bag on his lap. "Right. It's a 'sub' shop. I forgot that was their schtick. Funny. Well, maybe if he can't remember not to put tomatoes on your sub, he deserves a spanking."

"That's what bad boys get, huh?"

She held his gaze, her head tilting just the barest amount. "If that's what you're into. I suppose so."

*Is that what **you're** into?*

The words crested onto his tongue, a wave tasting of flirtation, and Joe swallowed them down without speaking. Why did he have to approach every woman like a conquest? Why couldn't he ever, just once, be a...person? Just a person, he thought, and the taste in his mouth turned so bitter he had to take a long drink of coffee to wash it away.

The woman seemed all right with his silence. She turned back to her own lunch, forking small bites of chopped salad with a delicate grace he admired as he fought with his own sloppy meal. When he muttered under his breath about the grease that had soaked through the paper to spot his suit trousers, she bent to pull a small package of wet wipes from her purse and handed it to him.

"You're very prepared," Joe said as he used the cloth to scrub away the stain before it could set.

"It's a very nice suit," the woman replied. "It would be a shame to ruin it."

Nothing about the conversation had been sexual. No innuendo. They'd barely spoken, shared no more than a glance or two. They were nothing but two strangers sitting on a park bench with their individual lunches, but that one act of caring from her, so casual, so bland, still sent a rush of heat through him with such ferocity he was sure it would scald her even across the short distance keeping them apart.

She looked at her watch and then tucked her napkin and fork inside the glass container, which she closed up with the plastic lid. She put everything into her bag and stood to sling it over her shoulder. She took up her gray woolen trench coat from where it had been slung over the back of the bench and hung it over her arm. Her smile, still, was impersonal, even indifferent, although her gaze moved all over his face and clearly took in every line and curve of it.

Joe stood too, the garbage from his lunch crumpled in one hand. He didn't offer the other, too aware that it was greasy from the sandwich. Their gazes met. Lingered. Her smile tipped infinitesimally wider. He smiled back.

"I'm Joe, by the way."

She nodded. "I'm Sadie. Nice to meet you."

Then she turned on her heel and left him. At the door leading from the atrium to the office building's lobby, she paused and looked over her shoulder. Gave him a tiny wave.

Joe waved back, and then she was gone.

TWO

For the first Friday night in a long time, Joe didn't go out. He stopped at the grocery store on the way home and picked up a steak and some greens for a salad, fresh veggies. He baked himself a potato and seared the steak to medium, sautéed some green beans and poured himself a glass of decent red wine. Not great red wine, but it would do for a night at home.

Alone.

He hadn't been able to stop thinking about the woman he'd met that afternoon in the atrium. Sadie. *Her name was Sadie.* He let himself murmur it aloud. An old-fashioned name, but he liked it.

Across from his dining room table, a large mirror hung on the wall. He'd put it there to make the space look bigger, not so he could admire himself, but now Joe twisted in his chair to make sure he could see every part of his reflection. He watched himself tip the glass of red wine to his lips. He watched himself drink. He watched himself lift the glass as though he were toasting the man in the mirror. The wine sloshed, splashing the back of his hand and the pale gray placemat he'd laid out on the table. He put the glass down, too hard.

It shattered.

For a moment, all he could do was stare in silence at the stem of the glass still upright in his fist and the shards strewn all over the table. They glistened, soaked with red wine that ran over the edge of the table and splashed onto his trousers. A wet napkin wasn't going to get them clean this time.

The wine glass had been a gift, a long time ago, from a woman who'd fancied herself in love with him. It had come in a set of four, and it was the only one that remained. She'd broken the first by throwing it at his head after he'd told her he didn't want to see her again. The second had been lost from the fumble-fingers of a different woman he'd brought home with him once; she'd had too much to drink and passed out in his bathtub, later. She'd been the last woman he'd ever taken back to his place. His cat had knocked over the third when he'd placed it too close to the edge of the counter. The cat had gotten loose some time after that and never came home. Joe had not replaced it.

He had only himself to blame for the loss of this last glass and for the multitude of jagged pieces now on the table waiting to bring blood. It was a good reminder to be careful, of how easy it was to break something even if you didn't mean to. Of how easily he could ruin something beautiful, simply by using it a little too hard.

You ruin things, Joe. You ruin them, and you don't even care. How can you not even care?

Joe closed his eyes and listened to the drip, drip of wasted wine hitting his hardwood floor. He could smell it, too, and the scent closed his throat up so tight that he could hardly swallow. He got up and, moving carefully to avoid the broken glass, took his plate to the kitchen where he put away the steak for another time. He got the broom, the dustpan, and a few slices of bread to pick up the tiny, unseen pieces of glass. He cleaned up the mess as best he could and left a note for the housekeeper to take special care in that room the next time she came in. Her name was Susan, and although she never cleaned anything exactly as good as Joe liked it, he didn't want her to cut herself.

In his bedroom, he hung his wine-wet trousers on a hanger and then on the back of the door, making a mental note to take them to the dry-cleaner first thing Monday on his way to work. He hung the rest of his suit back in its place in the closet, third from the left amongst the gray suits. He had four. He rolled up the tie and slipped it into its place in the drawer. Shirt, socks, and briefs he tossed in the hamper.

In the full-length bedroom mirror, he looked himself over again. Side to side. He turned to look over his shoulder at his back and ass, the backs of his thighs. Then the front again, his chest. Abs. His dick.

He could be hard in a few strokes, if he made the effort. Get himself off right here in front of the glass, watching his own face as he came. He'd done it before, on nights like this when the effort of finding someone to fuck was too much. Or, he could take a shower and go to bed early so it wasn't so difficult to wake up in the morning. He could head to the gym. Work out. Spend the day doing something useful with his time instead of recovering from another night of debauchery, trying to get the stink of a stranger out of his clothes or the taste of her off his tongue.

Orgasm or sleep? In the past there'd been no question, but tonight he chose the shower, twisting the handle but stepping in before the water had time to get hot. Shuddering, Joe took the pain, bending his head beneath the water and biting back a curse at the frigid stab of the needlelike spray as it raked over him. When it began to warm, he twisted the handle again to keep the water cold. Both hands on the tiled wall, he leaned to let the water batter him. It didn't help. By the time he got out, his teeth were chattering and goosebumps prickled all over his skin. His lips were blue.

"You ruin everything," he said aloud to the mirror. "Don't ever forget that."

THREE

Monday came, and he considered not taking his lunch to the atrium. January had been brutal so far this year, with snow and ice and bitter winds in regular succession. It would've been easier to stay in his office and close the door, to order something delivered right to him so he didn't have to brave the weather. He'd never know if Sadie had returned to the bench, or if she would look at him the same way she had on Friday — that was, as though he were just a normal person and not someone she wanted to devour.

"Hey."

The rap on his door tore his attention from the computer screen Joe had been staring at without really seeing it. He looked up. Smiled after a moment. "Sassy Blue."

The woman in the doorway laughed and entered. She gave a little curtsy, holding out the sides of her patchwork skirt and dipping low enough to jangle the series of silver necklaces around her throat. Today she wore her bright blue hair in a messy bun interwoven with strands of neon green and purple. Her real name was Sarah Roth, and she'd been working in the IT department for about half a year. Some of the partners complained that she didn't conform to their corporate standards, but Joe had seniority over them. If he said she stayed, she stayed...and he liked her. Sassy was always good for a laugh, but more than that, she was damn good at her job.

"I hear you got a virus from downloading weird porn again," she said.

"It's only weird the first time."

"Yeah, yeah, tell it to the next sucker." She shook her head with another laugh and gestured at his desktop. "Actually, I'm here to give you the software upgrade you've been promised for what, a month or so? It's going to take me a good forty minutes to get you all set up. I figured you'd be heading out to lunch about now, so it shouldn't interrupt too much."

His decision was made, then. Lunch out of the office. He grabbed a hot sandwich from the coffee shop in the lobby of his building and headed for the atrium down the block.

Sadie wasn't there.

Overhead, fog and condensation made patterns on the glass, and the winter-bright sun pierced its way through the shadows the small potted trees and Boston ferns were trying so valiantly to cast. The bench, the good bench without the splinters, waited for him. Joe sat and ate his lunch slowly, but by the time he was finished he couldn't think of any reason to linger.

There'd been no reason for him to believe she would have returned. In all the months since he'd started eating his lunches there, there were only occasionally other occupants. People walked through the atrium on their way to the food court in the office building on one side, or to the parking garage, or to the building on the other side, but they rarely stopped. It was what he'd always appreciated about the space. It wasn't hidden, but it was private. The small garden tucked between the two office buildings, accessible through the atrium, was the same. A pass-through, not a place for anyone to hang out.

She didn't show. He was disappointed, and he only had himself to blame. Quickly, irritated with himself for caring so much about something so small, Joe packed up his trash and dumped it. He pulled on his Burberry overcoat and looped his scarf — red cashmere today — around his throat. He pulled leather gloves from one pocket and smoothed them over his hands. It was a look that turned heads, and he did indeed get a double-take from a pair of young women dressed in scrubs who passed him on the sidewalk outside.

Joe made a show of pivoting on his heel to look at them, intending to give a low whistle that would make their day, but he pulled it at the last second when he saw they were no longer looking at him. It felt creepy to try and call their attention back after it had passed and arrogant to assume that they'd be flattered by a catcall from him. He caught sight of his reflection in a shop window and paused to give it a terrible frown.

"Your face will freeze that way, my mom always said." This came from the woman just stepping out of the store. "And listen, I know the prices are high but just think of how happy she'll be when she opens up the wrapping."

"Who? Your mom?"

"Oh, you're quick." The woman beamed at him.

He hadn't been paying attention to what was behind the glass, but now Joe focused on the mannequins displayed in the window. They all wore lingerie, one in cute boy-cut briefs with a skinny tank, another in a full Merry Widow corset, including the stockings and heels. The woman who'd addressed him rubbed at her arms, blowing out breaths.

"It's too cold out here," she said. "Come inside and see what's available."

Joe could already tell that *she* was one of the options — not for sale, but certainly rentable for a few hours. He imagined himself turning on his heel, perhaps with a jaunty "good day" or even a "be seeing you" complete with the weird finger-monocle gesture from that old scifi show, The Prisoner. He imagined himself not giving in to temptation, his *or* hers.

He went inside.

"Who are you shopping for? Wife or girlfriend?" The woman gave him a wink. "Or both?"

"Wife," Joe said. "Anniversary gift."

"Lucky woman. What year?"

"First." It was always so easy to lie that Joe sometimes had to wonder if he even knew how the truth would taste.

If the shopkeeper sensed he wasn't being honest, she didn't show it. Instead, she led him to a display of pretty nighties and matching panties. She didn't say anything about them, just looked at him looking at them.

"No," she said before Joe could make any kind of comment. "No, I don't think so."

He followed her into the back room beyond a beaded curtain that rattled and clattered as he pushed through it. The red-lit space featured a lot of animal print furniture and floor-to-ceiling shelves lined with clear storage boxes. The woman pulled one down and lifted out a diaphanous, pale-pink gown with a feather collar and cuffs. It was like something out of a 1940s film.

She held it up to herself. It wasn't her style. With her high-teased hair and swooping black eyeliner, she'd fit more into the sixties or seventies. Her body was lush, though, and he had no trouble imagining how it would look veiled only by the misty material.

"This," she said.

"I'm not sure," Joe answered. "I think I'd need to see it modeled for me before I could make a decision."

The woman's smile curved higher. "I thought you might."

She ducked behind a heavy velvet curtain, gown in one hand, and emerged a few minutes after that. Joe had loosened his scarf and removed his gloves, making sure to tuck them deep into his pocket to be sure he didn't lose them. By the time she was doing her slow twirl in front of him, he'd also taken off his coat.

He moved first; she expected it. Taking her in his arms, Joe tangled his fingers into the hair at the base of her skull. He pulled her head back, exposing the long line of her throat. Her body was warm against his, her breasts full and begging him to bury his face between them. He allowed himself the indulgence and lost himself, for the moment, in the soft crush and powdery scent of her cleavage.

Her hands slipped between them to caress the front of his trousers. "Mmm. Nice and hard."

It was true. It didn't matter that she was the sort of woman who didn't care if he didn't ask her name, or if a man was married, or even if he would respect her in the morning. She was warm and soft and curved and her mouth tasted like berries and her skin smelled musky, like secrets, and Joe wanted to discover every one of them. His body didn't care about what his head thought, and it definitely didn't give a damn about what his heart wanted. His body always understood what the rest of him struggled to comprehend — that sex could and did make everything all right.

At least for a time.

She let him press her down onto the leopard print chaise. With the gown pushed up over her hips and her ample thighs spread wide, she looked like a goddess, and Joe was ready to worship at her altar. He didn't have any protection, but there were other ways to make his offering.

"Oh," she said, clearly surprised when he settled onto the chaise and pulled her on top of him, then when he turned her to face away. "Oh, my."

Joe's first lover had referred to this position as "le soixante-neuf," and it was how he thought of it, now. Something foreign, something sophisticated and requiring skill, something intimate without requiring the burden of emotion. He could close his eyes and let her cries and the tense and release of her muscles guide his lips and tongue, and neither of them would need to speak.

Her orgasm happened faster than he'd expected, but the surge of it led to his own. They separated without clumsiness. She disappeared once more into the dressing room and returned fully dressed. She packed up the nightgown into a gift box and handed it to him, and he followed her out to the register. He paid cash.

"Stay warm out there," she said.

He held the gift box, now in a matching store bag, close to his chest. "I'll have some good memories to keep me from getting too cold."

"Who are you going to give that to?" She pointed at the bag.

Joe grinned. Shrugged. "My wife."

"Oh, *you're* not married." She waggled her fingers at him. "No ring, for one thing, but other than that...I could just tell. I have a knack for it."

"I'll have to find one, then. To give this to."

She laughed and gave him another wink. "Well, if you ever need anything else in the way of skimpy nightclothes, you know where to find me."

Back at the office, he set the gift bag on a shelf in his office. In his private washroom, he took care to scrub himself clean of any reminder of how he'd spent the last part of his lunch hour. He brushed his teeth. He studied his reflection but saw only the same old face.

Sarah waited for him when he came out. "I finished up your updates, but I wanted to walk you through the new password requirements. They're stupid."

"What would I do without you, Sassy Blue?"

"Suffer, I guess." She lifted a shoulder in an elegant shrug.

It took only a few minutes to get him set up, and when they'd finished, she stepped back to study his face. "Are you okay?"

"Sure. Of course. Why?"

She tilted her head to look him over with narrowed eyes and pursed lips. "You seem...never mind. Sorry. Forget I said anything."

"I seem what?" Joe swiveled his chair, his hands steepled in front of him.

"Sad. You seem kind of sad, that's all. Sorry," she repeated, sounding sincere. "It's really not my business."

Someone rapped on the doorframe, calling her name, drawing her attention away with an urgent IT need, and she went. Sarah paused, though, to look back at him through his doorway. Joe had not moved. He waited for her to say something else, but whatever she'd seen in his face must have been enough, because she only gave him a little wave and a sympathetic smile before she left.

You seem kind of sad.

Her words stayed with him for a long time, not because she was definitely right, but because Joe couldn't be sure she was wrong.

FOUR

February

The first Friday of the following month, Sadie had returned.

Her name rose to Joe's lips as he strode toward the bench, but he settled for smiling his greeting instead. She stood when he approached. Sadie was smiling, too.

"Hello again," she said. "Joe, right?"

"Yes. Sadie?"

"You remembered." She looked and sounded pleased.

They took places on opposite sides of the bench. She had another salad and a baguette. He'd picked up a chicken salad sandwich from the coffee shop.

"It's so nice in here, it's hard to believe how terrible the weather is outside." Sadie had taken off her jacket and sweater, revealing a sleeveless blouse that also showed off the curve of her collarbones.

Joe shrugged out of his overcoat and hung it on the back of the bench. "It's supposed to snow again by the end of the week. More ice, too."

"Oh, ugh." She frowned. "Did you lose power last week? We did. Two days."

We did.

His gaze dropped automatically to her ring finger, where she wore a small diamond alongside a gold band. "No. I'm on the other side of the river. Not as many trees."

"Lucky you. Green Street is lined with them. I love them, but they're all so old, they cause a lot of problems. So they top them," she added, her mouth twisting, "and that just looks ugly."

He knew the street she meant. Lined with older houses, many of them Victorian, it was in a section of the city that had once been considered "bad." Joe lived in a modern neighborhood on the other shore of the Susquehanna River. His apartment was modern and sleek and expensive but had very little charm.

"Kind of like me," he told her when he described it.

"Oh, I don't know about that," Sadie said. "You don't look so expensive."

Sun shone through the glass above them, but laughing with her was the real, true golden light. Nothing seemed artificial about it, or about her, and in that moment, nothing felt fake about him, either.

They might have sat on the bench and eaten their lunches in silence. Strangers, after all. He might have struggled to find a topic of conversation. She might have turned away a bit to keep herself facing from him. None of that happened.

Instead, they talked. About this. That. The other thing. Their favorite movies. Childhood memories of television shows long gone off the air. Books. She told him of her love for the smell of lavender, because it had been her grandmother's favorite, too. An hour passed, and then another, and he knew he should let her get back to work so he could return to his own office, but neither of them so much as hinted that they were late for anything else.

Years ago he'd had conversations like this with a woman. Not the first one he'd ever loved, although she'd been the first for other things. It had come as a shock to him when he discovered that most lovers didn't talk that way, in fact, that most people did not. Now here he was on a park bench with a woman he'd just met and had never even touched, and they'd already shared so much of themselves it was like they'd known each other forever.

Only when a cloud passed over the sun, sending their gold-lit sanctuary into gray dimness, did Sadie look up at the sky. A different sort of cloud passed over her expression. She frowned and looked at her watch.

"I really have to get going."

"Sure. Of course. I should, too." Joe got up when she did and held out his hands for her trash.

She gave it to him with a small chuckle and watched as he tossed it. "Thanks."

"You're welcome." He helped her on with her coat, too. Then put on his own.

They stared at each other, neither quite ready to leave. He was the first to turn on his heel and face the atrium's doorway. The first to take a couple of steps in that direction. To actually make the effort of leaving.

"See you," Joe said as he turned back.

Sadie smiled. "Next month. Yes."

Next month.

FIVE

March

The next month, Joe arrived before she did. Sadie wore lipstick, something he noticed but said nothing about. Again, they talked and laughed, and the time flew by quicker than a whore could squat, as his grandma would've said.

In April, they met in the atrium but together decided to move to the small garden tucked between the buildings, to sit beneath the hanging willow that cast green shadows in Sadie's eyes and rustled, whispering, as though it was laughing along with them.

In May, she brought a thermos of lemonade, homemade, she said. It was tart and sweet all at the same time, and when Joe complimented her on it, Sadie ducked her head and blushed. Then she looked him in the eyes and offered him another glass.

In June, it was Joe's turn to share a treat, and although he hadn't baked the muffin himself, Sadie had accepted it with a croon of delight. She'd brought him the book she'd told him about the month before, and in this small exchange of gifts they seemed to both take a step forward, if not together, at least in the same direction.

July was when everything between them changed.

SIX

July

The heat had been oppressive all week. The air conditioning had gone out in the office late yesterday afternoon when Joe had been putting more hours so he could be sure to have time for an extra-long lunch that first Friday of the month. It hadn't been fixed by this morning when he'd gone in early, and the other partners hadn't even bothered to come into the office. He'd given the staff the day off, something he knew Paul Gurney was going to get on his case about, but by this point, Joe had run out of fucks.

July was not a time to be at work. He should be at the beach right now. Cool breezes, hot sand, drinks in coolers next to beach chairs, women in bikinis. A book in his hand, shades on his eyes and nothing to worry about. He usually spent most of July in Delaware, "working from home" in the morning and hitting the beach all afternoon.

This summer he'd stayed right here in Harrisburg, and why? He told himself it was because the practice had grown so much over the past year that he needed to be onsite. He told himself it was because he was pulling his weight to make the business a success, because he wanted that end-of-year bonus. It was all bullshit. He was often more productive working from his house at the beach than he was in the office, and his annual bonus wasn't tied to anything but the bottom line.

He was staying home this summer because of Sadie.

She only ever came on the first Friday of the month, but Joe still went every day, just in case she decided to show up another time. He didn't want to miss her. Sadie seemed interested in who he was, not simply how he looked, and she was the first woman in Joe's life to act that way in a long time. He knew she was married, but they never spoke of it. They just...talked.

Like people.

Sadie made Joe feel like he was not just a man, but a *person*.

Six months shouldn't have been enough time to build a friendship that only had the chance to grow one day of the month, but theirs had. Now it was July, and there was heat and the lack of the ocean, and he was irritable, but there she was. Waiting for him on the bench that had become, somehow, "theirs" even though neither of them would have admitted it to anyone else or to each other. His bad mood dissipated at the sight of Sadie's smile, although there was no denying that she still looked sad.

"Everything okay?" he asked as he settled into his place next to her.

Today he'd brought a couple slices of pizza, not fresh. He'd ordered takeout last night, too annoyed with life to bother with making anything healthy. Pizza was fast, it came right to the house, and one pie could last him for a few days so he didn't have to cook or even buy groceries.

Sadie eyed the few slices he took out. Mushroom with black olive. She had a different lunch today. Instead of her usual salad and half a baguette, she'd unwrapped a turkey sandwich from the sub shop down the street. She also had a bag of chips and a bottle of cola. Usually she had a water bottle or a thermos.

"Fine. I'm fine. Everything is fine," she said.

It was a lie. Joe knew it the way he knew what she would bring for lunch, or if she'd like the book he was going to lend her, or if she would laugh at his stupid joke. What he was not certain of was if Sadie knew how well half a year had allowed him to understand her.

"How are you?" she asked before he could say anything else, her question a deliberate deflection to keep the conversation turned toward him.

"Horny." He gave the answer deliberately, a hard emphasis on the word. He wasn't sure why he said it. Until now, none of their conversations had so much as skirted that line. It hadn't even been true, not until he saw a flash of something in her eyes when she looked at him.

Sadie shifted on the bench, crossing her legs. Her skirt rode up to expose a bit of thigh, but she tugged it down at once. Not an invitation.

"I love women," Joe said. "I love the way their bodies curve. I love the way they smell. I love their moods, I love trying to figure out what turns them on, I love big tits, small tits, fat asses and skinny waists and thick thighs. I love everything about women and about fucking women."

Each word came out clipped, that same hard tone, but Sadie didn't even flinch. Joe added, "I love women, but I don't love *a woman*. So I settle for fucking them whenever I have the chance."

"And you have the chance a lot?" She phrased it as a question, but it sounded as though she already had guessed the answer.

"Yes. Always."

"You have a lot of one night stands?"

"Yes," Joe repeated. "Always."

"Tell me about the last one," Sadie asked.

SEVEN

POPPY

The woman I'm standing behind in the grocery store line has more than the allotted twenty items in her cart, but she either doesn't care or can't count, it's hard to tell which. Her long dark hair dangles in twisted knots to the middle of her back, and she's braided some of the twists with beads and pieces of ribbon, none of them matching each other or the strapless dress of gauzy fabric that hangs an inch or so too long. The hem is ragged from her stepping on it. She smells like coconut oil and pot.

"You want to go ahead of me?" She gestures at the conveyor belt already moving, lined with her items.

"No, that's fine. I can wait."

Her grin flashes white teeth in her deeply tanned face. She'll regret that when she's older, I think, all that time in the sun without protection. Or maybe she won't. She could be the sort of woman who will let her hair go naturally gray and wear her wrinkles with pride. For now, though, she's a wild thing in her mid-twenties who wears an ankle bracelet made of tiny silver bells. A woman who doesn't pay attention to signs and rules. One who ends up a few bucks short at the cash register.

"I got it," I say when she sighs and starts tallying things to put back.

Her smile is less grateful and slightly more calculating than it should be, but I'm the one who offered the money. "You sure? I can pay you back at the ATM."

"No problem." I can afford to be generous.

When it turns out she plans to haul her groceries home in a foldable shopping cart, I offer her a ride. This late in the afternoon the sun has been beating on the asphalt for hours. Wavy lines of heat rise up. The world's a pizza oven with the door open.

"Your ice cream will melt," I say like I have to convince her, even though she hasn't so much as hesitated at my offer.

Her name, she says, is Poppy. "It's on my birth certificate, in case you think I just made it up."

"You look like a Poppy."

"I know, right? Did you ever wonder if your parents named you something else, would you have ended up the same person?" She puts her seatbelt on without being prompted. I notice her nails are short and painted frosty pink. She wears a series of silver rings on her fingers, including both thumbs. Now that we're both in the car, close quarters, I catch a different whiff of her. Salty but less like sweat and more like the ocean. "Like if your parents had named you John or Henry or Roger instead of…what's your name?"

"It happens to be John Henry Roger."

Poppy bursts into tinkling laughter, the sound like the silver bells on her anklet. She throws her head back with the force of it. Slaps her thigh. When she looks at me again, her eyes, the color of sun-faded denim, are bright and full of the kind of promises girls have been making and breaking since I hit puberty…but Poppy definitely looks like she's also the sort of woman who keeps instead of breaks.

We go to her apartment, where I help by carrying her bags up the stairs. In her kitchen, she offers me a drink while she sorts and puts everything away. She gives me a beer, heavy and hoppy, not at all what I usually drink, but by the time she's put the last of her groceries where they belong, I've managed to drink the whole can.

She's the one who kisses me first, standing on her tiptoes to get at my mouth with her lush lips. Mine's already open. She swipes her tongue inside. Her hands slide up over my chest to link behind my neck.

"You," she says in a breathy voice, "are exactly what I've been craving."

It's as easy as that. It always is. I desire. I want. I crave, and I am craved.

Poppy strips out of her clothes and leaves them on the kitchen floor. Naked, she takes my hand, leads me to her bedroom. It's dark, the shades drawn. It smells like she does, the salty fresh stink of the sea.

If she were someone else, I might tell her about how much I've been missing the ocean, but those sorts of conversations are not for Poppy and John Henry Roger to have. The only thing they need to talk about is where to kiss, how to touch, which parts to stroke and which to bite.

"There," she says. "Fuck yes. There and there."

I press my teeth to the softness of her belly and dig my fingers into the meat of her hips and I run my tongue over her skin to get to the center of her, the sweet and seawater beginning of her, and I bury my face as deep as it will go to find every place that makes her jump and gasp and moan.

My cock is hard, but this is important work, the process of getting a woman to come. There are similarities from one to the next, but it's never exactly the same. Every woman is herself, unique, like a gift to unwrap or a puzzle to solve. I spend my time between her legs, licking, the pace steady even as her hips start to buck and she grabs at my head. The world goes dark and muffled when she clamps her thighs around my face, rocking upwards. Her clit's tight and hard and throbbing under my tongue, and she lives up to her name, blossoming just like a flower.

After, spent and gasping, she draws me upward and takes my cock in her mouth. It doesn't take me as long to come, not from any of Poppy's particular skill but because all I have to do is concentrate hard on remembering the sounds she made when she climaxed. How the flood of her juices covered my tongue and lips. How her body swelled and tensed. I come thinking about how good it feels to get a woman off, like an accomplishment or a trophy. I come thinking about how giving a woman an orgasm makes me feel good about myself, like at the very least, I'm worth something, like there's at least one thing in my life I don't always ruin.

BY THE END of the story, Joe's throat had gone dry and he had to stop and take a long, long drink. The cola in his cup was too warm and diluted from the melted ice, but it was all he had. He drained it, the straw rattling against the emptiness at the bottom of the cup.

Sadie coughed into her fist and took a drink herself. She screwed the cap back on the cola bottle, tight. "Why do you think you ruin things?"

"It's something in my nature. It's who I am. It's what I do," Joe said.

"No," Sadie replied, voice gentle. Calm. Low. Most of all, kind. "I mean, why do you *think* that about yourself? That you ruin things?"

He could have told her about Mindy and his brother and what had happened in the months before Eddie died, but the story he'd just finished had ended up revealing much more than he'd planned to. More than he would ever have intended, and yet it had come out of him on a wave of truth filtered through lies. Or maybe it was the other way around. There *had* been a Poppy. He *had* gone home with her. But it had been a year ago, and she had not been his last one-night stand. That one had been the roommate of a girl he'd met on a dating site, also last year, before he'd stopped bothering to answer all the winks and nudges that flooded his email. Roomie had slipped him her number while he waited for his date to finish getting dressed. He'd found the slip of paper in the pocket of his jacket last week.

"Why do you say things are fine when they aren't?" he shot back.

Sadie sat back against the bench, her formerly open expression shuttered and dark. A locked door. She gathered her trash and tossed it into the can before he could offer to help. She stood, facing him.

"Will I see you next month, Joe?"

"Do you want to see me, Sadie?"

She took two steps away from him. Ashamed, he noticed her fingers had curled into fists, and she was trembling. Her voice didn't shake, though, when she answered him.

"Yes. I want to see you again. Next month, like always."

"I'll be here," Joe said.

EIGHT

August

She wouldn't be there, Joe was sure of it. Last month, telling her that graphic sex story...there was no way Sadie was going to show up again. He'd so convinced himself of it that he almost didn't go to the park himself, and instead showed up so late that she'd already finished her lunch.

"I wondered if you weren't coming." Sadie stood as he approached the bench. Her voice wavered a little bit before she got it under control. "I thought maybe...never mind. Hi, Joe."

He lifted his soda cup toward her, then took a seat. After a moment, Sadie joined him. She didn't say anything as he unwrapped his sandwich, but when he turned to look at her, she was smiling. Her eyes were bright. She let out a small, embarrassed laugh and covered her eyes with her hand for a second.

"I was worried you wouldn't want to have lunch with me. After last month," she said.

She'd been worried? "What? Why?"

"I just thought that maybe you'd be upset. That I pried." Sadie shrugged.

Today she wore a light blue dress with a matching, lightweight cardigan and blue sandals. She'd done something different with her hair, too. Joe noticed, but of course he wouldn't say so.

"You didn't pry, Sadie. I put it out there. When you asked me to tell you, I wanted to. So I did." He hadn't had much appetite all day, and now it had totally vanished. This time, not from the anxiety of wondering if he'd totally screwed up the best thing that had ever happened to him, but from the anticipation of what she would say next.

"Why did you want to tell me about it? Something so personal?"

"Bragging rights?"

She shook her head. "I don't think that's it. You're not as arrogant as you like to pretend to be."

"Oh, I am. And even more." He settled back onto the bench, half-turning toward her so that their knees were almost touching.

In answer, Sadie only shook her head again and gave him a small smile. Her lips pressed together for a moment before her tongue dented the center of her top lip for a second so brief he almost missed it. She tilted her head, looking him over.

"Do you have another story for me?"

He did.

NINE

MARJORIE

I can't get enough of the ocean. If I go for more than a few months without the scent of salt air and the feeling of sand under my bare feet, I start getting tense. I don't care if it's covered in ice and snow, I need to get to the beach regularly, even if it's just a quick trip down for an overnight.

There are plenty of bars and clubs to go to, but Kokonuts is where it's at. From eleven in the morning to two in the morning, the club rocks non-stop. During the day, bikini-clad girls wander the sand floor of one bar section while dudebros in sleeveless shirts try to bump and grind with whoever they can reach. Last time I was here, I watched a girl in a white one-piece get fingered from behind while she gulped at a drink served in a parrot-shaped glass in front of the reggae stage. The guy straight-up stroking her clit never went under the fabric of her swimsuit, but he hardly had to.

At night, the club requires clothes, although many of the women here still wear what amounts to basically nothing. Short dresses showing off the curves of their ass cheeks, cleavage plunging in the front. In the indoor stage area, everyone sweats and grinds in one massive orgy while the cover band sings crowd-pleasers. Every so often, streamers shoot out of cannons in the ceiling and drop fluttering paper that tangles around ankles or gets stuck on sweaty, bared flesh.

If you want to get laid, Kokonuts is the place to be.

I'm just watching from my place at the railing between one upper bar and the lower dance floor. I've been sipping whiskey and riding a small buzz. Nothing heavy. I like people watching and the energy of the crowd. I drove here, and I'll face a good twenty minute ride home at the end of the night, so I'm pacing myself.

The woman dancing in front of me has long hair that the strobe lights show is dark auburn with some blond highlights framing her face. Unlike a lot of the women here tonight, she's not wearing anything too flashy. Her green dress shows off ample curves without showing too much skin, and while I'm certainly never too upset to take in the sights of women who like showing more, this woman keeps snagging my attention.

She has a great smile, I notice that. An animated face. She waves toward the dance floor and speaks to the man next to her, but it's clear they aren't together. Also clear that she's not trying to hit on him or anything like that. She's just...having fun, and I like that. I like fun.

When she whirls to face me, I'm sure she's got her eye on someone behind me, but I'm wrong. She crooks her finger, urging me to lean closer, over the railing. She's on the series of steps just below it, and she pushes up on her tiptoes to get close enough to me so I can hear her over the music. Even so, I miss what she says the first time.

"I said," she repeats, "I'm not sure if I'm in a bar or a zoo!"

"You're in a full-immersion safari experience," I shout into her ear. "Didn't they give you a safety vest and a dart gun?"

She laughs. "Good one!"

That's it, our moment has passed, and she turns back to shimmy and shake along with the song. I could keep standing here with my drink, or I could move around the end of the railing and find a spot next to her on the stairs. I think of how she talked to the other guy, earlier, friendly but not on the prowl, and my decision's made. It takes me a good five minutes to push my way through the even bigger crowd trying to get to the bar during the band's break, but I make it. I end up next to her, and at first she doesn't notice.

"Oh! Hey!" She says a moment later when she turns. "Jungle Jim."

"Jungle Joe." I hold out my hand.

She shakes it. "You can call me Marjorie."

"I can *call* you Marjorie, huh? So that's not your real name?"

"Nope." She grins unapologetically. "But that's what you can call me."

Marjorie moves a little in time to the music now being spun by a DJ, but there's not much room to dance. She finishes the last of her drink and looks around, but there's no trash pail within reach and finding one means braving the crowd. She waggles the empty cup.

"What are you drinking?" I ask. "May I get you another?"

"No, thanks. It's just water." She waggles the cup again and looks at my almost empty drink. "What've you been drinking?"

"Whiskey."

"Ah. Do you like it?" She taps her cup to mine.

"It's all right. Not the best." I swallow the last inch of golden fluid and tap her cup with mine, this time twice.

The band is returning to the stage, and Marjorie moves with the music, so I do, too. We end up dancing together after losing our place on the steps to a bunch of stumbling assholes, and I put myself between them and her to keep them from elbowing her in the head. She's a good dancer. So am I. But there's no real room here to do more than bop up and down.

We get closer, though. My hands on her hips. Hers on my chest. Lots of eye contact. We're close, our bodies aligned, but I don't grind against her. When the band starts with a slow song, everyone pairs up. Marjorie and I move a little closer.

A little closer.

She lets her cheek rest on the front of my shirt. Beneath my hands, one on her hip and other centered between her shoulder blades, her body is tense for a few measures. She relaxes. I pull her closer. We spin slowly in a circle, oblivious to the jackasses all around us.

The song ends. She looks up at me. "Would you like to walk me home?"

Home turns out to be a third-floor condo on the beach block, just a couple blocks away from Kokonuts. Outside the club, the night air is chilly, with a breeze blowing off the ocean the closer we get. She takes my hand as we walk and swings it gently, the way you do with an old friend or a longtime lover. We don't talk much.

Inside her condo, she offers me a drink, and I accept a glass of wine. She has one, too. At my raised brow, she laughs, looking adorably self-conscious.

"I don't drink out when I'm by myself. Too easy to get into trouble that way."

"Is this trouble?" I sip wine, then lift the glass to her.

"I hope so, Joe. Is that your real name?"

I put down the glass and take her hand to pull her, step-by-step, closer to me. "As real as yours is Marjorie."

I don't lie to protect myself. I'm getting the vibe that she wants anonymity. I can do that.

I lean to kiss her; she turns her face at the last moment. Her nervous laugh puffs soft, wine-scented breath. I don't move away. Our mouths are close, but not touching.

"I haven't kissed any man other than my husband in oh...twenty years or so." Marjorie draws in a hitching breath and steps away to look at me. "My divorce was finalized a few days ago. I got the condo."

"I'm...sorry?"

"You can say mazel tov, if you want to," Marjorie says. "It's been a long and miserable number of years, and I'm glad it's over. It's just been hard. That's all."

"I understand."

She's still holding my hand. I'm no longer sure this is going to end up in bed. Her fingers tighten in mine.

"Have you been married? Shit. Are you still married?" she asks.

"No, and no. I've seen a lot of divorces, though."

"Ah. You're a lawyer?"

I shrug. "When I'm not leading expeditions through the hookup jungle."

There. I got her to laugh, a genuine guffaw. Marjorie shakes her head and puts herself back into my arms. Her hands go behind my neck. She tips her face.

This time, she doesn't turn her head.

The kiss is slow and soft, and I try to make it one to remember. Her lips part beneath mine. Her tongue slips inside my mouth. When she moans, my dick twitches. She's breathing a little harder when she pulls away, and her eyes are bright, but I can't tell if it's from tears or arousal or maybe both.

"I went out tonight, just to see how it would be. You know? I figured I could walk down the block, have a drink or not. See what it was like out there. It was worse than I expected," Marjorie says dryly. "I am not sure I'm cut out for that world. But the dating sites seem even worse. And I'll be honest, Joe. I'm ready to be single, but that doesn't mean I want to go without sex. I haven't had good sex in half a decade."

"Would you like to have some tonight?"

"Yes," she breathes. "Please."

In her bedroom, I take my time undressing her. Her skin tastes of salt, but her mouth is sweet from red wine, and we kiss for a long, long time. Marjorie said she hasn't kissed anyone new in twenty years, and I want to make sure she gets enough of it, now.

Finally, she takes my cock in her hand. "I can't get pregnant. But would you mind...?"

"I always use protection," I assure her.

She sighs when I enter her. We kiss as I move. Her body welcomes me. I make sure to take my time until she's gasping out my name. When she shakes with her orgasm, I slow. Then I start again. She comes again, a little while later, and when I try the same trick, Marjorie laughs.

"No," she whispers. "I can't, again. I want you to come now."

After it's over and both of us have settled into a stupor on her bed, she turns to rest her cheek on my shoulder. Her hand on my belly. Her fingers trace small circles there.

"Thank you," she says. "It was perfect."

FOR A MOMENT after Joe had finished speaking, Sadie didn't say anything. She cleared her throat. She shifted on the bench.

"That's...it?"

"When she fell asleep, I walked back to my car and drove home. My place is in the next town. I didn't get her number. We never spoke again," Joe said.

"I meant...that's all there is to the story?" Sadie cleared her throat again and took a hasty sip from her water bottle. "I just...last month, it was more...explicit."

Heat kindled in Joe's stomach, low. "I wasn't sure you'd be into another super graphic story."

"It's not really my business, of course," Sadie replied quickly. She sat up straight and looked at her watch. "I'm late. I'll see you next month?"

She stood. Joe watched her. His heart thumped hard.

He opened his mouth to ask her to meet him next week and every week, but he stopped himself. Once a month seemed just right for this, whatever this was going to be. Whatever it had already become. Now he knew exactly what Sadie wanted from him.

And he was going to be sure to give it to her.

TEN

January, again

Something had started.

Every month, he told her a story.

Every month, she listened.

In the beginning, the stories were true and needed very little exaggeration. When did they turn entirely into lies, each of them? When had Sadie become the woman in every story — wearing a different name or face but always, always Sadie in his heart? Joe couldn't put a pin in that point on the map. He only knew that somewhere along this journey no matter how many side roads or detours he tried to take, the destination had become, and remained, Sadie.

A year passed and then another, one month at a time. The seasons changed. He and Sadie met on their bench in the atrium in bad weather and in the small park when the weather was fine. They never spoke or met up in the interim, although he'd seen her a few times walking on the street, her head up and gaze always so far away that he'd never once dared approach her. It might ruin their Friday lunch dates. He didn't want to risk it.

Today's story had been about a woman named Mary, a virgin who'd picked him up at a club. The story was mostly true, although as usual, he'd pulled the details from his past. The truth was that Joe hadn't actually slept with a woman in the past six months. Some days, he thought he might not ever have sex with anyone ever again.

"That's a nice story," Sadie said. "I like the part about how you made her a woman."

Joe reached for his paper cup of soda and took a long drink. Talking had made him thirsty. "Didn't I?"

"What I find interesting is the idea that a woman has to have sex to become a woman."

He shrugged and tore open the paper off his sandwich, pausing to pick off the hated tomatoes from it. He glanced at her. "Doesn't it?"

Sadie never interrupted him during the stories. She listened, intent, a flush rising in up the column of her throat and into her cheeks. Sometimes, her lips parted, and her eyes blazed. Sometimes, she drew in a small breath, a tiny gasp she tried to shield behind a cough. Joe tried to gauge the details he shared with her based on how aroused she seemed to be. Today he seemed to have judged wrong.

"I don't know what her problem was." Joe chewed and swallowed.

Sadie pushed a napkin toward him. "She'd just lost her virginity to a stranger. Maybe she felt awkward."

"She was on me like butter on a biscuit. How was I supposed to know she was a virgin? She didn't act like one."

"How's a virgin supposed to act?"

He didn't have a good answer for that. "I don't know. But she acted like she knew exactly what she wanted. So...why was she so upset when she got it?"

"Maybe she was disappointed."

He had to grin at that. All this time, all the stories. She knew better than that. "Sadie. I did *not* disappoint her."

"Oh, that's right. You made her a *woman*." She sounded annoyed. Again, he must have misjudged.

Joe frowned, less at Sadie's tone and more about how all of this seemed to be going awry. "You didn't answer my question."

"No. Losing my virginity didn't make me a woman. Did it make you a man?"

"I lost my virginity to Marcia Adams, my mother's best friend. It made me a man pretty fast. I wouldn't have survived it, otherwise."

That was a story he hadn't yet told her, and her expression showed her surprise. He laughed, one eye squinted, face tipped up toward the atrium's glass ceiling. He couldn't say he hadn't thought of Marcia lately. She was still his mother's best friend and therefore frequently the subject of conversation with his mom, who rarely asked Joe what he, himself, was up to. But he hadn't thought about Marcia in *that* way for a long time.

"Are you going to tell me about it?"

He shifted on the bench, uncomfortable about sharing it in a way he hadn't been about any of the other stories. "I was seventeen. She asked me to take care of her garden. Money for college. She told me I could use their pool every day when I was done mowing the lawn."

"Sounds like you did more than mow her lawn."

He rubbed a hand along the back of his neck. "Yeah."

"And you really think that's what made you a man?"

It both was and was not what had catapulted him out of his boyhood, but he wasn't able to explain to Sadie exactly how. Marcia had fucked him, but she'd never fucked *with* him. Marcia had been the one to show him the satisfaction of giving a woman pleasure before he took his own. She was also, so far, the only woman who'd ever seemed honest with him about what sex meant, versus what it was supposed to mean.

Joe shrugged. "Yeah. I think it showed me what to expect, anyway."

"I'm not sure that's the same thing."

"Well, if losing your virginity didn't make you a woman," he said, "what did?"

Sadie didn't reply to that.

Joe thought of the night with Mary. He'd done his best to make the sex good for her, and considering she hadn't warned him in advance that she was a virgin, he thought he'd managed pretty well. He'd tried to make sure she felt all right about it, after. She'd been the one to get strange about it.

"Mary acted like I was handing her a twenty and kicking her out."

"Maybe she assumed you were the sort of guy who picks up women in bars and sleeps with them, then expects them to leave." That cool, irritated tone was back. Haughty and kind of snide. She wasn't meeting his gaze.

"I'd have let her shower first!" he cried, indignant. "Jeez, I'm not a total asshole."

Yet he didn't deny he was, indeed, the sort of man who picked up women in bars and fucked them, perfectly satisfied with one night.

Again, Sadie didn't respond. Joe set his sandwich down, his appetite gone. The sun shining through the glass overhead cut through the giant Boston ferns hanging above them and covered Sadie's face in bars of shadow.

He frowned. "Say it. You want to. I can see it in your eyes."

"Say what?" She made a show of not understanding him. "That you *are* the sort of man who does that?"

"Keep going." He sat back against the bench, his arms crossed.

Sadie's smile held no warmth. "That you're a cheater? A rogue? That you don't know the meaning of fidelity? That you go through women like wind through lace?"

"Don't forget that I'm a silver-tongued devil who'll say anything necessary to get into a woman's pants. That my holy grail is pussy. That I've split more peaches than a porn star."

"Split more peaches? That's a new one." She laughed.

He loved Sadie's laughter and often drifted to sleep with the lilt of it in his mind, but not today. "Go on and say it, Sadie. I'm a manwhore. You think I'm a slut."

"Joe, stop."

"I know you think it, so you might as well say it."

"But Joe," she said gently. "It's true."

"It won't always be true!" His words rang out, echoing.

How could she look at him and not see that? All of these months, every story, all of their conversations…how could they have turned out to mean nothing? Because they *were* nothing, he thought in a fury. At her. At himself. Because he'd been filling her head with fantasies about the kind of man he was, and he'd covered up all of his truths with all of those lies. Sadie believed he was that kind of man because he'd convinced her of it.

And why had he done it? To stop himself from pursuing her. To protect her from his once-and-done habit with women. He'd done it so he didn't ruin this.

"Oh, please." She sounded angry, too.

He stalked toward her, expecting her to back up. Sadie didn't move. He leaned in so close he could have kissed her. In her eyes, that familiar flash. The wanting, the craving. For the first time since they'd met, Sadie looked at him the way every other woman ever had.

"It's true," he said through gritted teeth.

"I've heard that before. But every month you come back here and tell me a new story about some new woman. Or more than one. So you'll have to forgive me if the idea of you suddenly becoming Mr. Faithful sounds a little funny, when every month it's another new story."

He'd meant for her to back away, but he was the one who did. "Every month, you listen."

"Is it my fault you have stories to tell?"

You ruin things, Joe. You ruin them, and you don't even care. How can you not even care?

"I don't have to prove myself to you," he said.

"No." Sadie clenched her fists, then with an obvious, conscious effort, relaxed them. "So why are you trying so hard?"

"What about you? What are *you* trying to prove?" Joe demanded.

"Me? I don't know what you mean."

"Why do you listen, Sadie?"

She fussed with her trash, turning away. They'd never argued, never shared a cross word. Yet here they were, fighting like lovers, except that he'd never so much as kissed her, and if they'd ever even touched, he could not think of the occasion, now.

"Not so nice when it's turned around on you, is it?"

She twisted to look at him. "I've been listening to your stories for a while now, Joe. I guess it's just become a bad habit."

He had given her the ammunition, and now she used it to shoot him. "Bad habits should be broken, though, right?"

He turned on his heel and stalked away.

"Joe!"

He didn't turn back.

ELEVEN

February, again

Despite all the stories he told Sadie, Joe actually did have some small measure of self-control. His six-month, self-imposed dry spell had ended, though. He could say it was because he was horny and the opportunity presented itself, but the truth was that their January conversation had prompted him to go out looking. The encounter with the random girl he'd met out dancing had been sexy, like something out of porn film, but it had left him hollow. He hadn't even asked her name. At home, later, he'd had to admit to himself that he'd only done it so he'd have a story for Sadie.

He told it to her without embellishment. He couldn't look at her when he did, afraid she'd see from his expression how he really felt about it all. He twirled his straw paper in his fingers, knotting it.

"Why didn't you ask her name?" Sadie asked.

Finally, he twisted to face her. "Because it didn't matter."

Emotions rippled across her expression. He'd done the right thing, telling the story, making sure she knew the girl meant nothing. This friendship between them had become based on an image of who

Sadie believed he was. What was more important to him? Changing, or continuing on as they'd begun?

He didn't know.

"About last month. I'm sorry," she said.

He shrugged. "You were right."

Sadie looked away.

"I wasn't even planning on going home with her," he said after a minute, because although he was a liar, the truth was begging to come out. "Or with anyone."

"So...why did you?"

"C'mon, Sadie. You know how it is."

"No, actually. I don't."

Joe let a puff of air seep from his lips, not quite a whistle. "You've never?"

"No. Never." She shook her head.

"You've never been with someone only once." He wasn't sure if he envied her or did not believe her.

"I've only been with one man."

Shocked, Joe said, "Only one."

"Yes."

He did believe her, and he didn't envy her. "Good for you."

"You're avoiding the question," she said with a laugh. "If you weren't planning on going home with someone, why did you?"

"Because I could. Because she asked. Because...I always do."

Joe took a drink while Sadie unwrapped her lunch.

"Haven't you ever done something just because it's easier to do it than not?" he asked.

She replied at once. "Of course."

"Tell me."

"It's not as exciting as your story, Joe."

He smiled, leaning forward. "No? That's too bad. Tell me, anyway."

"When I was growing up, my sister and I fell into these...stereotypes, I guess you could say. I was the smart one. She was the pretty one. We kept it up through college, and I guess even now. It's stupid, but you know how families are."

"Try being the disappointing one."

Sadie studied him. Today he wore a blue shirt. His favorite dark gray suit.

"Oh, you aren't," she said. "You can't be. Look at you, Mr. Successful."

He shrugged again, still smiling. "My parents aren't impressed with fancy suits and expensive ties."

They'd talked a bit about their families. She knew he had a sister who was married with children and a brother who'd died. This was the first time he'd spoken about his parents.

"As far as ties go, it's a very nice one. Even if they don't like it, I do," Sadie said.

Joe ran a hand over it. "Yeah? You're impressed by this tie?"

"Keep in mind my knowledge of men's couture is pretty limited."

He stroked the fabric. "I like this one, too."

The silence between them was no longer awkward.

"Sometimes," Joe said after a bit, "it's just easier to keep being what everyone expects you to be. Even if that's what you're not, anymore."

She nodded in agreement. "I wasn't sure you'd be back, after what I said."

"I thought about it all month. Just not showing up."

"So...why did you?"

He told her the truth. "Because it was easier than staying away."

TWELVE

Joe had lived in this house for his entire life until moving out at age twenty. He still knocked at the back door to the kitchen like a "tradesman" as his mother would say. The maid opened it for him.

"Hi, Vera."

"Hello, Mr. Wilder. Your mother's in the dining room arranging the flowers." Vera stepped aside to let him in with a nod of her head.

He found his mother exactly where Vera had said she would be. Cut flowers and large crystal vases covered the large dining room table, which was big enough to comfortably seat ten without the leaves and twice that when they'd been added. He stopped himself asking what the flowers were for just before he could make an utter ass out of himself.

"They've asked me if I would mind if we changed the memorial service to this Saturday instead of Sunday, since the baptism is this Sunday. Of course I said yes, and they'll use the same flowers. I'm happy for them to."

"The baptism?"

"For Angel's new baby." His mother looked over the rim of her glasses at him. "Don't tell me you forgot."

Joe could admit to that, since forgetting a baptism for his mother's best friend's grandchild was a far less egregious offense than forgetting the memorial service for his dead brother. His mother sighed and wagged a finger at him. He countered with a grin that was meant to be charming, and must have been at least a little, because she chuckled.

"You forgot," she said. "Well, you'll be there, of course. You can't miss it."

"I wouldn't miss it for anything." The truth was, he hadn't seen or spoken to Angel in a decade. He wouldn't even know her if they passed on the street.

"You know Marcia always asks about you." His mother fussed with a vase crammed with white daisies and some kind of blue flower. She paused for a moment, keeping her gaze on the arrangement. "And of course you'll be at Edward's memorial."

"Of course. Unless Dad doesn't want me there."

She whirled. "Don't be a child, Joseph. Of course your father wants you there."

Joe said nothing.

"That was one time, and he wasn't well. And you must admit, you'd been terribly abrasive to him." Her voice wavered, but her chin lifted. Her version of the story was the only one that counted.

"I'll be there," Joe assured her to counteract any tears that might come.

Before Eddie died from leukemia at seventeen, Mom had been full of good humor. Not afraid of getting dirty, working for hours in her garden without even bothering to wear gloves. She'd coached Joe's baseball team when he was a kid. She'd taught him how to cook. She'd played a mean game of pinochle and liked a good naughty limerick, and she'd been proud of him, of Joe, the son she'd used to call "her golden one." Her younger son's death had stolen the light from her eyes. Joe saw a hint of it sometimes when she played with his sister's children, but nothing Joe could ever do was able to bring it back for him.

They never spoke of how he had betrayed his dying brother by knocking up Eddie's girlfriend, or of the abortion his father had given him the money to pay for. Mostly, Joe's parents never spoke to him at all. Never anything beyond the most basic pleasantries, anyway. Never anything real.

"Did you stop by for something in particular, or...?" She let the question trail off vaguely, already turning back to her flowers.

"Just to make sure you didn't need any help for the service. That's all."

"Not a thing." She offered her cheek for a kiss but didn't look at him. "See you Saturday."

He'd been dismissed.

EDDIE'S memorial service was brief, as it was every year. Anything too long would have been "vulgar," according to his mother, but Joe had always thought the amount of preparation she put into the flowers and the food for such a short service made the event unnecessarily ostentatious anyway. It had become more about seeing who showed up — or who did not — rather than anything to do with his brother.

He hadn't expected to see Mindy Heverling there. She was Mindy Goodman now and had been for at least ten years. Joe had not been invited to the wedding.

Mindy looked good. Heavier than she'd been in high school, and she'd let her hair grow back naturally dark, but her bright smile had always transformed her face from pretty to blinding beauty, and that had not changed. She carried a girl toddler on her hip and an older little boy clung to her hand. There was no sign of a husband. Maybe she had come alone.

Joe watched her greet his mother from across the room. The women hugged, cheek-to-cheek, the embrace a little too long. When they parted, Mindy's eyes were red, and the little boy holding her hand looked up at her with concern. Joe couldn't see his mother's face, but he suspected she was not weeping. She never did in public.

He and Mindy finally met up at the folding table laden with sandwich platters and bowls of deli salads at the back of the church hall. Joe had not sought her out, but when he turned around with his plate of food, Mindy was there. She smiled at him.

"Joe. Hi. It's been a long time."

He nodded and bent to look at the little boy now clinging to Mindy's leg. "Hi, there. What's your name?"

"That's Chance. This is Delia." Mindy set her daughter on the ground next to her son. "How've you been?"

"Good. You?"

Their casual small talk had no meaning to it, but the warmth in Mindy's gaze said more than words ever could have. Her children helped themselves to cookies from the trays while she kept watch but allowed them to do it without assistance. She stepped in only when Delia dropped hers on the floor, but Mindy dusted it off and handed it back before there was so much as a single shed tear.

"They look like you," Joe said.

Mindy laughed. "Only people who don't know their dad say that. They're both really miniatures of him. But thanks for saying so."

"He's a lucky man," Joe said and meant it.

"And what about you? Is there a lucky woman?"

"There's a woman," Joe replied in a light and easy tone, although the words themselves were hard to say. "But I don't think it's ever going to amount to much."

"That's too bad. You deserve to be happy, Joe."

The room was clearing. Across it, near the door, Joe's mother and father were saying their goodbyes to the lines of people who'd showed up to pay their respects, not to Eddie whom most of them had never even met, but to Joe's parents. His mother looked up and saw Joe talking to Mindy, and her gaze burned him even from this distance.

"It was good to see you," he said. "You take care."

Mindy took a quick step forward. "Joe. Wait."

He waited, keeping an eye on his mother.

"I just wanted to tell you that...well, we never had the chance to talk, really. After. And I just wanted to let you know that I never blamed you. We were both there. We were both responsible. I'm sorry you got the worst of it all."

"I should have been there with you for it, at least." He pitched his voice low, to keep others from overhearing. "I owed you that."

"I know your parents didn't want you there. I knew it back then. I was just...upset." Mindy's lips quivered, and she pressed them together. "But I never blamed you, not really. We went to college and..."

"Lost touch," Joe said.

"Yes." She sounded relieved. "We lost touch."

"Do you want to keep in touch now?" He looked again at her children, their mouths ringed with crumbs. At the rings on her finger, the shiny diamond and gold.

She hesitated. "No. I don't think that's a good idea. I just wanted you to know."

He would have hugged her then, maybe even pressed a kiss to her cheek. Friendly, nothing more. A forgiveness and a parting.

They had an audience, though. His mother, her expression twisted into a frown and her hands clutched in front of her to still the anxious workings of her fingers. Joe stepped away from Mindy.

"It was good to see you, Mindy. You take care."

She breathed out, a sigh that sounded like relief, and Joe realized that for all of these years, Mindy must have thought she somehow needed to ask for his exoneration, and for all of these years, Joe had thought the same about her. She gathered her children and gave Joe a small wiggle of her fingers as she herded them away. He watched her go and wondered briefly what she would do if he went after her, but in the end, he did the right thing and let her walk away.

Minutes later, in the church hall now thankfully empty of anyone but Joe and his parents, his mother hissed accusations at him through the tears she must have been holding back the entire time.

"How could you. How dare you!"

Joe didn't bother to defend himself.

"It's all your fault. If you'd been able to *control* yourself, those children would have been my grandbabies, Edward's legacy." His mother broke into strangled sobs. "If you'd just managed to keep it in your pants, Edward might have had something to live for…"

"Now see what you've done. You've upset your mother." Joe's father, eyes red but from whiskey, not from weeping, spat the words.

Joe didn't point out that Eddie and Mindy had never been guaranteed a happy ever after, even if Eddie had never gotten sick. Nothing he said would matter, so he said nothing. His father looked him over, up and down, with a twisted look of disgust.

You ruin things, Joe. You ruin them, and you don't even care. How can you not even care?

His mother had railed those words at him at Eddie's first memorial service, and he'd carried that accusation with him ever since. She'd never said it again, but then, she'd never had to. She let out a low moan and sagged against his father.

"You're a disgrace," his father said. "After all these years, still such a disappointment."

"That's me. Nothing but a loser."

"You don't. Even. Care," his mother gasped.

Ah. There it was. Joe didn't argue. He just left.

THIRTEEN

April, again

The next day, he'd gone to the baptism. His parents expected it, no matter what had happened after the memorial service. Joe had let Honey Adams, the daughter of the woman who'd taken his virginity, jerk him off in a hedge maze. It hadn't been amusing at the time, but he'd told the story with an edge of humor, hoping to make Sadie laugh, and it had worked.

Maybe they could get back on keel.

"Everywhere you go," Sadie said when the laughter again had died down. "How do you do it?"

Joe had reveled in her laughter, but now he was quiet for a moment or two. "I'm a good-looking guy. It opens doors."

"You don't always have to say yes, Joe."

"Sadie," Joe murmured. "I don't always say yes. I only tell you about the ones I say yes to."

More laughter, this time sounding less honest. The hour had passed, and although some days they spent longer than that here on the bench, today it was clear she intended to go. He wanted her to stay, so he tried honesty.

"They're like sharks. Circling. Cute, single guy, good job, nice car. It's all they know about me," Joe told her.

"Maybe because it's all you show them."

"Maybe it's all they want to see."

She stood, preparing to leave. "Maybe you need a mesh suit. Or a shark cage. Or maybe you just need to stop tossing out so much chum."

"Then what would we have to talk about at lunch?"

"So, what was the rumor about you and Mindy Heverling?"

Honey had mentioned it, and Joe had added it to the story. Had this been the story he really wanted to tell Sadie, all along? Joe thought it might have been. "Mindy was my brother's girl."

"And?"

He ran a hand through his hair and shifted on the bench. They'd covered rough topics before. Sadie had a way of digging deep. Analyzing. Joe had done his own digging to discover she was a psychologist, although he never told her that he'd looked up where she worked or where she lived.

"Never mind," she said. "You don't have to tell me."

"Eddie was a year younger than me. He was the smart one, I guess you could say." Joe's laugh caught in his throat, thinking of what she'd told him about her sister, the pretty one. Sadie had been the smart one. Roles they'd taken on for some reason, whether they fit or not.

"And you were the pretty one?"

"You got it," he said.

"So, what happened?"

Joe leaned forward, elbows on his knees, hands linked. He'd never told anyone else this story. "She got pregnant."

"Oh?" Then, after a second. "Oh. Oh!"

Joe nodded. "More like, 'oh, fuck.'"

"What happened?"

"She had an abortion. I had to borrow the money from my dad to pay for it. He told me I was a disappointing bastard, and he was right. Eddie never knew about it. By then he was sick. He had leukemia. Anyway, he...died."

"I'm sorry."

"It was a long time ago."

"Joe," she said softly and waited until he looked at her. "I'm still sorry."

He wanted to tell her the rest of it. Of what his mother had said then, and how his parents had treated him forever after that. About seeing Mindy at the service and how much of a relief it had been to know she didn't hate him. That was the story he ought to have told her, not the one about Honey and the handjob. Too late now. The story had been told. Their time was spent.

"Thanks. Oh, I almost forgot." He stood and pulled a tissue-wrapped package from his inside suit pocket. He held it out on the palm of his hand. "Happy Birthday."

The package tipped from his hand and missed hers, hitting the ground, where Sadie bent to pick it up with a hasty apology. "You didn't have to get me something. I hope it didn't break."

"I think it's okay. Open it."

Joe had never been big on celebrating his birthday, but when he'd learned that only a few days separated his and Sadie's, he'd made a note to remember. He'd bought the pale purple hand-dipped candle from a local boutique. It smelled distinctively of lavender. She sniffed it with her eyes closed.

"How did you know?" Sadie asked.

She never spoke of her husband, but her question told Joe a lot about what her marriage had to be like. "You told me. You said it was your favorite scent."

"I did?" Her answer said even more about her marriage than the question had. "Really? It is, actually."

Joe smiled. "I thought you did. Anyway. Happy birthday, Sadie."

"Thank you." With a funny grin, she reached into her bag and pulled out a book, the latest hardcover thriller from a well-known author. "Surprise. I hope you don't already have it."

"I don't." He didn't mention it was probably going to be the only gift he received.

Sadie smiled at him, and Joe smiled back. They both lingered, not standing close enough to touch yet somehow embracing. He imagined pulling her against him for a hug — a way of saying thank you between friends, who would fault him? Would she? In the end, Joe instead took a few steps back before turning on his heel and walking away.

FOURTEEN

May, again

Why did people ever bother to get married, when all they did was end up fighting over who got to keep the good set of pots and pans?

It wasn't the first time Joe'd had that thought, especially after working some of the more complicated and bitter cases he'd been mediating. The partners gave him the difficult clients, the ones who didn't seem capable of getting their shit together. Usually he didn't mind. Those couples had paid for his house at the beach.

People got married because they thought it was what they were supposed to do. But why did people *stay* married when being married made them so miserable? Sadie had looked sad again today. She'd smiled as usual when he arrived at their bench, but it didn't reach her eyes, and there was no hiding the shadows beneath them. Flowers were beginning to bloom after the long winter, but Sadie was withering.

This month's story was, once again, mostly lies with some bits of truth. He *had* been in a wedding. He *had* gone to a strip club, but they hadn't been alone. The rest of the bridal party had been there, too.

He *had* fucked the bridesmaid in the car, though. That part was true. He'd done it hard and fast. She'd been wet from the lap dances and the flirting, and her clit had been tight and swollen under his fingertips as he stroked her. She'd come in under five minutes...and he hadn't. He didn't tell either the bridesmaid or Sadie that, of course.

When men fucked, they came, every time, or something was wrong.

Wearing a condom meant he didn't need to explain anything to the bridesmaid. He'd simply disengaged, handed her a tissue from the center console and moved over to the driver's seat. She'd seemed a little embarrassed by it all, and although Joe wished she wasn't, it had been hard work on his part to act like it had been all in good fun. Because it should have been, he thought, and wanted to tell Sadie the truth. All of it should have been fun and sexy and carefree, and instead he'd gone home thinking about how little pleasure he'd actually taken from that encounter.

"So what happened at the wedding?" Sadie asked, bringing him back to the bench and the reminder he was telling her a story.

"It was fine. Every time I looked at her, she started to giggle. We held it in pretty much during the ceremony but at the reception she got toasted and couldn't stop laughing."

"You know, for someone who claims he's not a slut, you sure don't prove it." She looked annoyed.

Could he blame her? How many stories had he told her, all of them with a different cast of characters, aside from himself, but all of them with the same ending. He could protest, but that didn't change anything.

"Sadie," Joe said finally, trying to explain, "she lives in another state. It was a wedding hookup, that's all. Happens all the time."

"To you. Not everyone in weddings hooks up." Her chin lifted the tiniest bit, and her eyes flashed at him.

Joe could get annoyed, too.

"What, I should've gotten her email address? Promised to keep in touch? She didn't even pretend that's what she wanted."

"You could've resisted the urge to fuck her in your car."

"But why?" When she didn't answer, he continued, "Sadie, she wanted to do it. Nobody got hurt. I was careful. I'm always careful. What's the big deal?"

He studied her as he waited for her answer, uncertain what he hoped she would say, only knowing that it would not be what he wanted to hear. That it would sting. And that it would be the truth.

"You say you want to settle down. Find someone. But you just keep fucking your way through woman after woman. *That's* the big deal. I think you're full of shit."

In all this time, they'd never fought about anything. Now within a few months' time, she was angry again about the same issue.

"And I think you're being a judgmental bitch."

Her jaw dropped before she closed her mouth with an audible snap. He leaned against the back of the bench, arms outstretched along it, and gave her a practiced smirk he knew would read as smug. Distant. He was putting on a stranger's face to keep her from seeing how upset he was.

"I don't hurt any of them, Sadie."

She sniffed. "So you say. All I ever hear is your side of it."

"Would it be better if I pretended I intended something I don't? If I took them out on lots and lots of dates, got their hopes up? Would that make me a better person?"

"How do you ever expect to find someone if you never give them more than one night? If you 'been there, done that' to everyone?" Sadie tossed up her hands, exasperated.

Joe drew in a breath and sought to meet her gaze, but Sadie wouldn't meet it. "Maybe I'm looking for something special."

"Well," she said stiffly. "How do you think you're going to find it if you keep hopping in and out of beds all over Harrisburg?"

"It was in a car," he pointed out, but his humor fell flat.

"The point is, Joe, you say you want something, but you show no intentions of making any sorts of lifestyle changes to support it."

He sat up straight. "You make it sound like I fuck every woman I meet."

"Don't you?"

Joe leaned forward a bit more, his eyes dark and his mouth curved downward. This time, she did meet his gaze, and he held it. Silent at first, before his answer came in a low, strained voice. "No, Sadie. I don't."

He had never fucked *her*.

She knew what he meant. He knew she did. But neither would acknowledge it, or what it meant…or did not mean. Instead, they turned back to their sandwiches and drinks and finished their lunches as though the entire conversation hadn't even occurred.

FIFTEEN

SASSY

I've never considered himself technologically challenged, but no matter how many times I tried to upload this file to the server, it continues to crash. I fought with it for twenty minutes, muttering curses under my breath. When the knock came at my door, I'm ready to bite the head off anyone who dares interrupt me.

"It's a virus, it's nothing personal," Sassy says, although I haven't so much as let out a word about my troubles. "Half the practice got it."

"It's set me back a day's work. Damn it. I told Paul we need to update the virus protection."

Sassy laughs and pats my shoulder. "Never fear. Sassy's here. I'll have you back up and running in no time."

"If you can do that," I tell her, "I'll buy you dinner tonight."

Sassy flirts with everyone; I've seen it. She flirts with me all the time, and I usually flirt back, but we've never taken it farther than that. I didn't mean anything with the offer of dinner, other than appreciation. Yet later, sitting across from her while we both sip glasses of very good red wine, I have to admit that Sarah Roth might be my match.

Not like a romantic partnership type of match. More like she's the first woman I've met in a long time, since Marcia Adams, actually, who seems fully capable of straight-up making me an offer of a string-free fuck...and more than that, convincing me both that she means it and that she's capable of sticking to the part about there being no strings.

Across the table, she lets her gaze linger longer than it needs to. Every now and then, even over the smells of garlic and oil and fresh bread, I can catch her subtle scent. A perfume I can't name, but it wafts its way through every nook and cranny I have, and I'm uncomfortably semi-hard in a couple of minutes.

"You're so beautiful. I'd love to sketch you," she says.

"I didn't know you were an artist."

"I'm not, really. Art's something I do for fun. It's not my career."

"You don't have to make a living at it to be considered an artist." I lean across the table toward her so I can fill her glass again from the bottle we've almost emptied.

Do I want to do this? It's no seduction, unless maybe I'm the one being seduced. I like Sassy, but I don't want to lose her amazing IT skills. She's the only one the firm's ever hired who can actually get the job done.

Do I want to do this because she's made it clear she's willing, that there are no further expectations, because I always do it, because I am that guy, the one who'll take it wherever he can get it?

Do I want to do this because Sassy, at least, wants me?

The rest of the dinner passes quickly. Shared dessert. Discussion about books. She's easy to talk to, but I knew that already. She says she'll catch a cab home, but I offer to drive her. If she says yes, I think I'll go to bed with her. Sarah says yes.

In her kitchen, which has been remodeled with retro appliances, she pours me another glass of wine. I know the brand. It's expensive and very, very good. This and the way she's clearly spent time and money to turn this house from wreck to showplace, show me a side of her I've never had the chance to know in the office.

"The previous owner went to live with her son. It was in pretty bad shape. I've been refinishing it myself. I'll sell it at a profit in a year or two," she tells me when I ask her about the changes she's made to the house.

"That makes sense. This doesn't look a house for a Sassy to live in."

"Most people live beige lives," she explains in the bare living room, where paint cans and brushes still scatter the tarp-covered floor. "I want to sell this place to a nice upwardly mobile Yuppie couple, if they still exist."

I think of how many of my colleagues and acquaintances would fit that description and laugh. "They do."

Sassy has a great smile, but she's not using it now. Instead, she assesses me. I've seen that look on her face before, when she's deep-diving into something that's gone wrong with my computer. She studies and considers, figures out the problem. Then she fixes it.

I wonder what she thinks she can fix about me.

When she finally speaks, her voice is sweet and low and already husky. "I don't live in most of the house. But upstairs, in my bedroom..."

Our eyes meet, and for some long minutes, neither of us moves.

"I'd like to see it." I sip the last of my wine.

I give Sassy a good old grin, the kind that's meant to make me the Moses of women's thighs, parting them with my staff. Inside, it feels like flipping a switch. Something shifts in my dick, but also in my brain. I'm still here, focused, and yet there's now a distance I didn't feel earlier, at dinner, or even just a few minutes ago in her kitchen. I'm flirting. I want to fuck Sassy, with her blue and green hair and the black polish on her nails and the slippery slow way she slides her tongue along her lower lip, telling me she's as serious about this as I am.

"Then c'mon upstairs," she says with a crook of her finger.

I take a step closer and settle the glass on the newel post. Sassy takes my hand and links our fingers together, so I follow her up the steep and narrow stairs to the second floor. She pauses at the door I assume leads to her bedroom.

"Sassy." I take a length of her hair between my fingers to toy with the blue and green and purple strands. Her hair is soft. I imagine it falling over my belly and thighs while she goes down on me.

"Joe." She wiggles her eyebrows at me, teasing.

She's fun. This should be fun. But... "Maybe I should go."

My hand is still held tight in hers. She doesn't let me go. Without turning, she pushes open the door behind her and pulls me into her bedroom.

"Do you *want* to go?" she asks.

"No."

"So then don't." Sassy pins me with her gaze, and I want to lose myself in it.

I really do. Instead, I look around her room. She's really made this space as special as she is — deep blue walls and ceiling with a matching deep blue carpet. Small specks of luminescent paint in the shape of constellations cover the walls and ceiling. Her bed's just a stack of mattresses on the floor, covered with dark blue blankets, but I bet it'll work just fine.

"Wow." Still holding her hand, I turn around as far as I can before I look back at her. "You *are* an artist."

"Thanks," she says, her tone pleased.

We are doing this. I pull her closer. She's tiny, but not small. My hands fit just right on the curve of her hips, and for now I'm happy to keep them there. She tugs at my tie, loosening it until she can pull it free of my collar. She unbuttons the next button of my shirt.

I know she wants this, and my cock wants her. No question about that. Still, I put my hand over hers. Maybe to stop her. Maybe just to slow her down. I don't know. I don't know much of anything, anymore.

"Sassy, wait..."

"Shh. It's okay. This will be fun, I promise." She waits a second or so, her brow furrowing. "You're not gay, are you?"

Of all the questions I imagine she might have asked me, this is not one of them. "No! Why? Do I act like I'm gay?"

"No." She slides the next button free. "But you'd have to be gay to turn me down."

She's funny and delightful, and I laugh. "I'm not gay."

"Joe, sweetie, listen. I don't know what kind of girls you're used to, but let me make a guess, okay?" She says this as she swiftly finishes undoing my shirt and folds it open to bare my chest to her warm, soft hands.

They all think they know me. None of them ever do. I think that Sadie's come the closest, but even she has no true, real idea of who I am. "Okay."

"You like women. You're not as picky as a guy like you could be, and that's not bad. It's a good quality. But you're looking for something in particular, which is why you keep looking, am I right?"

I shiver at the slide of her fingertips around my nipples. "Yes."

I can't recall the last time a woman undressed me, but Sassy does. She takes her time, tugging my shirt free of my trousers slowly and carefully before she slips her palms up my chest to my shoulders. She slides the material free, leaving me shirtless. I shiver again, my skin prickling into goose pimples. I swallow, hard, and fight the urge to kiss her.

I fight it because I want to kiss her, but also because once I do, this will change. I will take charge of her, and of this, and I'll go distant again so I can lose myself in the pleasure of it all. So I can push myself into focusing on the physical sensations, without having to...well, fuck. Without having to *feel* anything.

I don't love the woman in front of me, but I do like her and respect her. This is meant to be only a one-night thing, and I think we're both more than okay about that. I just don't want to be the one to fuck it up. Sassy deserves better from me than that.

"You're not a player. I was wrong about that." She gets on tiptoe to nuzzle at my skin.

"I'm not?" Her hair…thick and smooth, with all those colors…I can't stop myself from gathering it in my fist and tugging it.

She counters with a lick, and I'm the one who makes a sexnoise.

"No," she says. "A player is someone who sets out to fuck his way through women without regard to their feelings. A player gets off on getting what he wants and then leaving. A player gets off on the escape. But you, Joe, you…You want to be caught. Don't you."

She cups my cock through my trousers. I pull her hair, tilting her head to look at me. She lets out a hiss. I've been too rough, too hard, but her words hit me hard. She strokes my cock through the fabric, and we stare each other down until at last I concede and loosen my fingers in her hair.

"It's not that simple, Sarah."

"It never is."

My cock is in her fist before I know it. I groan as she dry strokes me. "Sassy…"

When I look at her, Sassy brings my hand to her breast. I'm surprised to feel the bite of metal through her nipple as it stiffens through the fabric of her shirt, although the fact she has her nipple pierced shouldn't be a shock. I am suddenly, fiercely fucking aroused.

This is what sex is about. This is why I do it whenever I can. For the moments when the body takes over and I can't think of anything but getting inside something warm and wet, of touching and stroking and getting a woman off. Of getting off, myself. So I can get lost for a while.

We move toward the bed, where I stop to push down my pants and briefs. She's taking off her own clothes, both of us moving fast and fumbling but still efficient. We're naked in a minute or so, and I let myself admire her body.

"Smug appreciation," she says. "I'll take it."

"What?"

"Your smile. Smug appreciation. You're a man of many smiles, Joe. I've seen smarmy charming, sincere humor and reluctant wistfulness. Now I've seen smug appreciation."

I think about this as I cup her luscious breasts and rub my thumbs again over her nipples and the rings there. I don't like this assessment of me, but is she wrong? I don't think so.

I try again.

"How's that one?"

"Very nice," she says with a nod and maybe, just maybe, a little smug appreciation of her own.

"*You're* very nice." It's an old joke, one my brother and I shared. She won't get it, and I don't want to be thinking about my brother right now.

Instead, I move my hands over her body. I cup her asscheeks, round and firm and sexy. She pinches my nipple again, and fuck, yes. I like that. It's been a long time since I've been with someone who keeps up with me the way Sassy does.

"Don't sound so surprised," she says. "I might not be the sort of girl you're used to—"

I align our bodies, skin to skin. I'm hard against her stomach. "And I'm your type of guy?"

"Not really. No." Her voice is hoarse.

Good.

"Too clean cut? Not enough ink?" I trace the tattoo on her belly, an intricate Celtic knot surrounding a Star of David.

"You got it."

I want her on the bed. I want her nipple in my mouth. I wonder how the metal will taste. So I find out.

"Funny, I thought I'm any woman's type," I say in a low voice.

"Is that your problem? They all think you're their type?"

I've been letting my lips roam over her body, especially the sweetness of her throat, but now I pause. Here is a moment for lying. But I don't.

"Yes." I bury my face against her neck.

Sassy runs her fingers through my hair. Stroke, stroke. It's different than the touch of her fingers on my cock, but I let myself sink into it anyway.

"Poor Joe. They all want you but none of them know you." Sassy takes my face in her hands and looks into my eyes. "Why don't any of them know you?"

I have so many answers for that, but none make sense. The only one I could say that she might understand is that it's my fault. It's always mine. I ruin things.

"Sweetie, it's all everyone's looking for. Someone to know them." Sassy's voice is soft and gentle.

It's too much, and she must sense it, because she releases me. I want to leave, but after a few breaths in and out, I let myself relax against the warmth and softness of her body. I press my lips to her throat so I can feel her heartbeat. Sassy runs her fingers over my back, up and down, again and again. Her body enfolds me, and, because I can't stop myself, I let myself be embraced. My heart pounds. My cock's still hard, that not-so-little bastard.

"How many women?"

"A lot. Too many. Not enough."

"When's the last time someone took care of you?"

I can't answer her. We hold onto each other, tight and then tighter. Two ships tossed in a storm...no...only one ship tossed. I am the ship.

Sassy's fingers trace my spine. "Roll over."

I do at once. So many women, all this time, and it all comes back to the first one, doesn't it? The one who ordered, the one I obeyed.

She turns off the light. The stars she's painted all over this room glow. I would never do something like this to my house, but here, with her, I let myself love it.

This is how we fuck.

Sassy touches me; I touch her. She nips and bites, and this, like the universe she's made of her bedroom, I let myself love. My hands find all her curves and softness. When she bites me harder, I grunt and my cock gets impossibly harder. She is above me with her knees pressing my hips and her hands next to my ears. When she bends to sink her teeth into my flesh I can't hold back my cry.

"Shh." Sassy hushes me and kisses the spot she stung with her teeth.

My cock is hard and throbbing from the small pain and the weight of her body on mine. From everything we are doing and everything I want this to be, but I know it is is not.

Her hair, that glorious hair I admired before and imagined draping over my cock, trails over my face and arms as she kisses down my chest. Again, Sassy takes one of my nipples into her mouth. She bites it, and my entire body jerks.

Her soft laughter sends another rush of heat straight to my dick. "Sorry."

"...Jesus, Sassy."

"Should I be more gentle with you?"

I'm not sure what I would say if I was able to speak, but she bites me again and any words I might've found are lost.

Sassy uses her mouth on me for a long time. Every time I get close to the edge, she eases off to keep me from going over. It's a sweet fucking torture, but I give up to it without protest. Her fingernails dig deep, every now and then, and I welcome every little ache she provides. I think of Marcia just once before I push away the memories. It's rude to think of one woman while your dick's getting sucked by a different one.

She pulls a condom from the bedside drawer. She slides it onto me, and it takes everything I have to hold back from coming right then. She fits her body onto mine, taking me in all the way. She tweaks my nipples, hard, and again I have to fight from exploding.

She moves on me, rocking slowly like waves. But not on the ocean. A lake, a pond. Something still, but deep. It goes on forever. When I thrust too fast, she grips me with her thighs until I stop. She bites me, licking the spots after. I want to know if she's close, because I can't tell, I'm too close myself. I'd feel worse about it, but Sassy's made it very clear that she's in charge here.

At last she rides me harder, writhing and crying out. Her body tightens around me. Only when the tension in her eases do I let myself finally come. She falls forward, her face against my neck. Her hair covers me, as soft and fragrant as I'd always imagined it would be.

"Why don't you have a boyfriend?" I ask after a while.

"That's a million dollar question." She taps my chin with her fingertip. "I don't want one right now, I guess. I'm not looking for one, anyway. I mean, I guess I wouldn't turn one down if life threw him in my lap, you know? But I'm not trolling."

"You're not like most of the women I know, then."

"Honey, if I had a nickel for every time someone told me that, I'd be able to retire."

I want to go to sleep her with her next to me, but I know I won't. Even if I doze off, I'm not going to stay here the whole night. I never do.

"I mean, most of the women I meet want a boyfriend. They might say they don't. But they all do," I say.

"Well, sure they do. Most people, if you ask them, want someone. Nobody likes to be alone."

"They see a suit and a car and a job."

I didn't mean to tell her that.

"And you see tits and ass and hair."

She didn't say it like an accusation but I tense. "Yeah. I guess I do."

We yawn at the same time.

"Tell you what, bunny," Sassy says. "Stay here tonight and get some sleep, and in the morning I'll make sure you're up and out the door in plenty of time to run home and get ready for work. I'll even make you eggs."

"You will?" It sounds so nice. It sounds like something anyone would want.

"Sure. Turn over."

I've never been the big spoon. I can't sleep this way. I can't stay here, with this woman who seems like she wants to take care of me. She's taken care of me all night.

JOE FINISHED THE STORY, watching Sadie's expression the entire time. She was trying to hide her anger, but he could still see it even when she acted as though she was intensely interested in her sandwich.

"So, did she make you eggs?" Her casual tone didn't fool him.

It wasn't right to take joy in this, but he was. He leaned back against the bench and stretched out his legs. "No. I woke up before she did and left."

"So...are you going to see her again?"

"I see her almost every week," he replied, deliberately obfuscating.

"So, it's going well for you."

"She comes into work, that's all, Sadie. I haven't gone out with her again."

"Why not?" Sadie put down her sandwich and concentrated on the soda, sucking so hard the straw rattled the ice in the cup.

"Because she's not my type, and she's not looking for a boyfriend, anyway." He paused. "I like her."

"There's nothing wrong with liking her," I answered crisply. "She sounds very likable."

She wouldn't meet his gaze, but he studied her anyway. The story he'd told had been more than a sexcapade. Surely she had to see that. Right?

"What do you see, Sadie? When you look at me? Am I just a suit and a car and a job?"

She didn't answer for what felt like a long, long time. "No."

"Look at me, Sadie."

She did.

"What do *you* see?"

She shook her head and cut her gaze from his again. "I should be getting back. I have an appointment in half an hour."

It had been stupid of him to even ask, to think there could be any answer from her. He tried to laugh, but what came out was more like a hoarse gargle.

"See you next month," he said.

She nodded, still not looking at him. He didn't get off the bench. Many times they left the bench at the same time, but most of the time, Joe was the first to walk away. Not today. Today, he sat and waited for her to look at him. To say something, anything, that gave him even the barest hint of what she thought about him.

But Sadie only walked away.

SIXTEEN

July, again

Joe had met a woman.

Her name was Priscilla, and she was everything someone like him was supposed to want. Successful. Beautiful. Classy. Smart. He'd met her at a party for mutual friends. He had walked her home and left her on her doorstep without so much as a kiss goodnight.

If Sadie had been jealous of his story the month before, this month's had her looking sick to her stomach.

He'd thought about lying to her. After all, it wouldn't have been the first time he'd exaggerated the details in order to get a reaction out of her. He could have said he went inside Priscilla's house, fucked her. He could even have said he spent the night with her.

In the end, Joe decided the truth would be harder for Sadie to hear.

And he wanted her to hear it, didn't he? He wanted her to know that just because he'd spent the past couple years telling her, every month, about his sexual conquests, that didn't mean there weren't *any* women out there who had the possibility of becoming more than one-night stands. Joe wanted Sadie to hear that maybe, no matter what *she* thought, Joe might actually be ready to settle down with one woman.

It might even be the truth.

Although none of his monthly tales took a long time to share, this one had been shorter. He'd told it while sitting straight up on the bench, staring ahead. One word at a time, no embellishments. Finished, he waited for her to speak. When she didn't, he did.

"Ask me, Sadie."

She shook her head.

"Ask me why I didn't fuck her." He continued staring straight ahead, very aware that she was staring at him, but she'd done her share of not looking him in the eye. He couldn't bring himself to look in hers, now.

"Don't you want to know?" Joe asked.

Sadie said nothing.

"I've seen her three times since then." He did not say this to dig at her, although he was aware it might. It was simply the truth. "I'm seeing her again tonight."

Say something, Sadie. Tell me not to. Something. Anything.

And then, *you ruin things, Joe. You ruin them, and you don't even care.*

He did care, though. Too much. He cared so much about ruining this that he'd deliberately made several dates with Priscilla so he could be sure to have something to tell Sadie the next time they met.

At last, she spoke. "Why didn't you fuck her, Joe?"

"Because she's different." He looked at her. "Don't you want to know why she's different?"

Again, Sadie shook her head. "No, Joe. I don't."

Once, Marcia had told him that love and hate were different sides to the same coin. You could hardly have one without the other. Joe had never really understood what she meant, not really. Not with his heart, anyway.

He did now, because he hated Sadie.

He hated her for being unhappy in her marriage but not leaving it.

He hated her for not wanting him enough to say so. For making him want her too much to risk losing her, and this, and them, and the possibility that there might, someday, be something more than a once-a-month meeting on a park bench.

He hated her because he loved her.

He stood. A young mother holding a child by the hand crossed the path in front of them. The boy toddled with determination, almost falling once but deftly caught by his mother. Both Joe and Sadie watched them until they rounded the corner and disappeared.

"Have a good time tonight," she said then, her voice firm. Sincere.

This had to end, and he would have to be the one to end it. Not that it had ever started. With a nod, still not looking her in the face, Joe walked away.

SEVENTEEN

August, again

Joe did not ski. He had when he was younger, because skiing was just the sort of sport his parents supported, unlike wrestling or football, both of which his mother had declared "vulgar." Joe no longer skied because he hated the feeling of plummeting down a mountainside, sheer drops on either side, two thin waxed planks on his feet the only thing keeping in place. He'd never so much as broken a bone, and he could navigate double black diamond trails. He just hated it, the feeling of being out of control and vulnerable.

This thing with Priscilla had started making him feel the same way. He'd started it. He could keep up this relationship, but he felt the same way he did at the top of a mountain — a small push would hurtle him down at breakneck speed, and he wasn't sure he was going to be able to make it in one piece.

Priscilla, on the other hand, had made it very clear that after the number of dates they'd had, that she expected him to step up his game. She'd laid it all out for him. Her plans. Her desires. She hadn't hesitated, even once. She hadn't really asked him what he wanted, either.

She'd initiated sex, and it had been fine. She had a beautiful body, and she knew it. She hadn't demanded much from him. If anything, she'd seemed to think she was the one doing him some kind of favor, giving him a treat.

Joe had told Sadie all about the date that had led to this discussion between him and Priscilla, and what it meant. When he was done telling the story about how Priscilla had negotiated her way into full-fledged girlfriend status, he forced himself to look at Sadie. He wanted her to look stricken. Upset. He wanted to see the loss of him in her gaze, to see that she knew what she had lost, even though they'd never had anything to start.

He wanted his words to hurt her.

If they did, though, she was keeping it so close to herself that he couldn't be sure. She'd been like that in the beginning of this, hiding her feelings behind careful neutrality, but fuck, there'd been too many times now that she'd let him see her. See who she was, what she wanted. Why else did he make his stories so detailed, so outrageous?

It was all so he could get to Sadie.

All of those stories were about women to whom he'd given different names, but the truth was, all of them were and had always been Sadie in his mind. When he wove her a tale of sex and lust, when he watched her cheeks flush and the way her tongue slipped along her lips to wet them, when he knew she was getting turned on by him, it was worth every exaggeration…every lie, he had to admit. Every lie he'd ever told her.

But this story about Priscilla had not been a lie, and that was why he'd closed the bedroom door without sharing the truth of what had gone on behind it.

"You don't think I can do it, do you." This was not an accusation. It was an appeal.

Sadie looked at him, her expression serene, and no matter how hard he searched her gaze, he could find no hint of tears or rage or anything but calm. She'd gone away from him, and he'd pushed her there. Too late now, too late to take any of it back, to shield the truth with a different fiction. He'd fucked up, not for the first time in his life, but maybe for the worst time.

"That's not my place to say," Sadie told him in that calm and soothing psychologist's voice.

He hated it.

"You know more about my sex life than anyone ever has. You know more about my life than anyone ever has," Joe said.

He had trusted her with more about him than he'd ever done with anyone, but how could he say, so, now? How, when he'd just told her all about how he'd made a commitment to another woman for the first time? He and Sadie had shared multiple first Friday lunches. For more than a dozen stories of fiction occasionally spiced with some truth, the one thing the two of them had never, ever done was admit that this was anything more than a once-a-month thing.

Maybe for her, that was all it had ever been.

"If you're asking me to make judgment—" Sadie began.

"I'm asking you to tell me if you think I can do this." Joe kept his voice courtroom cold. Steady.

"That's not up to me to say, Joe!"

Finally, he'd managed to get a reaction out of her. They'd turned to face each other, not even close to touching, and still the distance was too close. He needed there to be more between them. He needed to be so far away from her there was no chance of him reaching for her, which is all he wanted to do. All he'd wanted to do since almost the first time they'd met.

She was waiting for him to speak, but Joe couldn't find any words to give her. He saw her struggle then, but could take little comfort in watching her expression crack. Her mouth worked and she drew in a long, deep breath before she finally spoke.

"No. I don't think you can do this."

Then tell me I don't have to.

Of course she'd say no such thing, not even after all this time. He looked at the ring on her finger, the plain thin band of gold that had marked her from the start as nothing more than an impossible dream. If he kissed her right now, she would let him. She would open her mouth for him and give him her tongue, but she would hate herself for it. Worse, she would hate him.

She should hate him, though. She should never want to see him again. Every time they met, there was a new and greater yearning between them. In the beginning the ache had been vague, more a sense of dissatisfaction in his life that went away when they were together than anything more. Over time, it had become desire. Longing. It had become everything he'd ever wanted and all he knew he did not deserve.

Sadie was another man's wife. She was not, and never would be, meant for him. Joe sat forward on the bench, his elbows on his knees. He looked at his hands, clasped together, then back at her.

"I think you're wrong." He got up. He tightened up his tie and put his jacket back on.

"I hope you're right, Joe."

He looked at her so long and hard it burned. "Well. We'll find out next month, won't we?"

EIGHTEEN

September, again

Joe could have told himself that it was mere coincidence that Priscilla had decided to surprise him today, the first Friday of the month. He knew better. He'd mentioned, speaking so casually that he knew she would notice, that sometimes he met a friend for lunch on this day. He hadn't said a name or even that the "friend" was a woman, but Priscilla knew. Didn't women always know?

He could have insisted that the two of them find some other place to eat lunch. Priscilla, after all, hadn't so much as said a single word implying that, when she'd arrived with a lunch for two, she intended for him to take *her* to the bench. She would never have tipped her hand that way, but Joe knew it. Didn't he always?

The sound of Sadie's footsteps on the gravel reached him before the sight of her did. When she saw him, or more likely, when she saw the woman next to him, she caught her toe on a rock and stumbled a little. Priscilla turned her head. Joe didn't get up. He put an arm along the back of the bench, and Priscilla moved closer.

It *had* been about Sadie, after all.

"Are you all right?" His voice was neutral. The sight of Sadie's flinch should have filled him with angry joy, but it only stabbed him in the tender place between his ribs. "Watch your step."

"They really should clear these paths more often," said Priscilla, her voice serene and confident. The threat had been assessed and dismissed. "You could have turned your ankle."

"I'm sorry. I didn't realize this bench was occupied."

Priscilla glanced at Joe with narrowed eyes. "We could move over…"

"No, that's fine." Sadie declined quickly, already backing away. "I'll find another one."

"Are you sure?" He traced the back of Priscilla's neck with one fingertip. "There's room for one more."

Both women looked at him, their expressions nearly identical. Joe could not bring himself to feel ashamed, although it was obvious he'd been caught out.

"No. Thank you. Enjoy your lunch."

For one second, the briefest of moments, Joe and Sadie's eyes met. Her voice hadn't even trembled. She might have stumbled when she arrived, but she wasn't anywhere close to faltering now as she walked away.

"Was that your…friend?" Priscilla's titter was meant to sound light, but Joe heard the bitterness beneath the light trill.

"No," Joe said. "She's not my friend."

NINETEEN

October, again

Why did people ever get married?

Because it's what they thought they were supposed to do.

Joe had not actually been unfaithful to Priscilla, at least not so far. The story he'd brought to Sadie this month had been entirely made up, exaggerated to the point of ridiculousness. Three women at the same time? Hookers, at that? She had to know it wasn't true, but she seemed to think it was.

"Do you want me to say I told you so?" She sounded triumphant.

He managed a smile. "Do you want to say it?"

"No."

He waited for her to ask him why he'd brought another woman to this bench, which had always been and was always supposed to be his and Sadie's. He'd been the one to insert the reality of their lives into the fantasy they'd been sharing for a couple years, now. Still, Sadie hadn't pointed that out.

"No?" He cocked his head, his smile growing wider. *You don't care*, he thought and tried hard not to. "You're sure?"

"Is that what you want? To say I knew you couldn't do it? I knew you'd never make it last?"

He'd worn the tie she liked today. Her gaze dropped to it now. Sadie looked him in the eyes. He said nothing.

"Fine," she said coldly. "I told you so, Joe. I knew you'd never be able to make it last. I knew you'd never be able to be faithful. But that doesn't matter anymore, because this is over. It's done. I'm not coming back here again."

He nodded, incapable of anything else.

"No more stories." Sadie sounded as though she was fighting tears, but her face was implacable.

"No more stories," Joe agreed.

It had come to this, the way he'd always known it would. Something good had been broken and ruined. But this time...was it really his fault? Or was it simply a necessity, the end of something that had never been meant to go on?

"Good luck, Joe."

"Thanks, Sadie." He stood, facing her. "I'll need it."

Sadie looked stricken. He leaned in close, lowering his voice. If she had meant to be the one who ended this, he wasn't going to let her. It would be him.

"I asked her to marry me, Sadie. And she said yes."

TWENTY

Appointments with caterers, florists, dress-fittings, cake tastings. Priscilla had planned out her wedding long before she'd ever met Joe, but that was fine with him. He didn't care about the color scheme, or a theme, or even how much it all cost. His parents loved her. They were giving him enough to cover the expenses of the sort of affair his mother approved of, and Priscilla's own parents were doing the same. Everyone was thrilled about this marriage.

Almost everyone.

"Darling, I was thinking about lilies for the centerpieces. Those pink ones. You know the ones I mean." Priscilla paused to eye the glass of wine Joe had ordered. "You know, I was also thinking about both of us doing a cleanse before the wedding. To be sure we're in our best shape. *Joseph.*"

Her sharp tone was meant to draw attention back to her, but Joe had been caught by the sight of someone else. Sadie. She looked gorgeous. She wasn't alone.

The man in the wheelchair looked tall and as though he'd once been broad, with big features. He was having a hard time maneuvering the chair through the crowded restaurant because rather than moving out of the way, people seemed set on ignoring him. Sadie was murmuring "excuse me" to each of them, but her voice sounded tense and her expression looked the same way.

"Pardon me," Priscilla said as she shifted her chair so Adam could get by.

Sadie wasn't looking at Priscilla. She was looking at Joe.

"Thanks," said the man in the wheelchair as he attempted to pass Priscilla.

This was Sadie's husband, Joe realized. She had never said a word about him being disabled. Did that explain why she's seemed so sad so often? It had not been a bad marriage, after all, just one under strain. Shame curdled in Joe's gut as he thought of his hatred, his anger, of the times he'd pushed her buttons to suit his own twisted desires. He was worse than arrogant. He was a monster.

Sadie broke the gaze first. She put her hands on the back of her husband's wheelchair, perhaps trying to push him faster. There was no way she could. The space was still too narrow.

"Sadie, hold on," her husband said, irritated. "Wait a minute, someone's got to move or something."

Red crept up her bare throat and into her cheeks. She let go of the wheelchair and clenched her fists, but not before Joe saw her hands shaking. There was nowhere for any of them to move.

"Here." Joe stood, moving with easy grace, and tapped the oblivious man at the next table on the shoulder. Fuck that guy, pretending he didn't notice any of this, when all he had to do was get off his ass and move his chair. "Can you move, please?"

It took only a minute or so to clear the way, and Joe did it quickly and quietly so as not to draw any more attention. He bent to pick up a fallen napkin, in case it might get caught in the wheelchair's wheels. Then he stood back, out of the way, to give them room to pass.

"Thanks, man," the man said.

"No problem. Have a nice night."

"Joe, darling," said Priscilla from behind him, her voice sharp. "Sit down."

Joe waited until Sadie and her husband had moved several tables away from them before he did. Priscilla gave him a stony look. When he drained half his wine and gestured toward the server for another, she lost her patience.

"I wish you wouldn't," she said, then paused. "Did you…was that someone you know?"

"No," he lied. If she remembered Sadie as the woman from the bench, she wasn't giving any hint of it, and he wouldn't have put it past her to have dismissed Sadie as competition so thoroughly that she did not, in fact remember.

"Oh. Good." Priscilla pressed manicured fingertips to her chest. "I'd hate if we had to change the wedding venue to accommodate that chair thing. Can you even imagine? How horrible it must be. Living like that."

"I can think of more horrible things than that," Joe said.

TWENTY-ONE

February, once more

December had passed in a blur, followed by January. Cold and dreary and depressing. Joe had gone to the bench, same as always, but Sadie never came.

Then, February.

"It's good to see you, Sadie."

She'd made an obvious effort at dressing up, doing her hair and makeup, but she still looked smaller. Worn.

Joe's heart ached at the sight of her.

"I figured you weren't going to come back," he said.

"My husband had a stroke," she said quietly, looking toward him at last. "He died."

She staggered, and he reached for her.

"Do you have a story for me, Joe? Because I really need one."

He had a story. Not one he'd expected ever to tell her, and not one he particularly wanted to share, but how could he deny her?

He told her everything. How Priscilla had ended things, thinking she could somehow control him. How surprised she'd been to discover that her threats didn't work. That he'd been relieved it was over.

He thought Sadie might scold him, and he would have deserved it. She didn't. She sat quietly next to him on the bench. Their shoulders touched.

"You can say I told you so," Joe said.

"No. I don't want to say that."

"She didn't know my middle name," he said. "Or my favorite color. Or anything about me, really."

"Why didn't you ever tell her?"

"She was happy with me the way things were. She didn't seem to need to know those things."

"But...you knew them about her. Did she tell you? Or did you just pay closer attention?"

He sighed. "It doesn't matter, now."

"Will you tell me something?"

He looked into her eyes. "Sadie. I think you know I'll tell you just about anything."

"Did you want her to not know?"

"Are you asking me if I wanted to fail?" Joe asked her.

"Yes." Their hands were close together on the bench, not touching, but close. "Did you?"

"I didn't think so at the time."

"Someday, Joe, you're going to run out of stories."

There was so much more he wanted to say to her, but for now, this would have to be enough.

He laughed, shaking his head, and got to his feet. "I don't think so. See you next month?"

"I don't know. Maybe not."

Joe put his hands in his pockets and rocked on the balls of his feet before answering. "I hope I do, Sadie. I really do."

They both smiled. Hers was still tinged with sadness, but she looked a little brighter than she had when she got there. Because of him, he hoped. Maybe he'd made a bit of difference.

"Thank you," she said.

Joe leaned closer, just a hair. "You're welcome."

They left at the same time but headed in different directions. Joe stood on the corner, surprised when Sadie showed up a few minutes later in the same spot. It was the first time that had ever happened. They both laughed, self-conscious, before parting again.

He turned at the last minute, thinking he'd call out to her, but she was already gone.

TWENTY-TWO

The overpowering scent of Stargazer Lilies was giving Joe a headache. So was the overwhelming variety of perfumes worn by his mother's friends, all of whom had seen it necessary to draw him into lingering hugs as they murmured their condolences over the ending of his engagement. It was more than his own mother had given.

His parents were celebrating their fiftieth wedding anniversary, complete with a catered meal, a band, and dozens of their friends. His sister Rachelle had put together a slide presentation that constantly circled through a range of photos. Joe's contribution had been to pay for the flowers.

"You're not drinking champagne."

The familiar female voice rose the hairs on the back of his neck, and he turned, already knowing who he would see. His mother's long-time best friend. "Marcia. You're looking well."

It was not a lie. She wore her silver hair as a choice and wore it well. She leaned to let him give her an air-kiss, and Joe half-closed his eyes, expecting the scent of suntan oil and chlorine. She smelled instead of something lighter and fresh, but the perfume still dragged at his temples and made his throat ache.

She lifted her own crystal glass to perfectly painted lips and sipped. "Your mother lost her mind about what happened. But how are you taking it?"

"Things don't always work out the way we'd like them to," Joe said, but paused to add as he looked into her eyes, "but then again, sometimes, they do."

Marcia laughed. Crimson liquid swirled inside the much larger bowl of his glass as she tapped her champagne flute against it. "It's always been my belief that marriage should be the last resort."

"I wouldn't say that too loud, if I were you. This isn't the audience for it." Joe waved his fingers in the general direction of the room, full of older couples lauding his parents for the accomplishment of their marriage.

Marcia gave a low, throaty laugh. "Come have a cigarette with me."

"I don't smoke."

"Come with me anyway. Keep an old lady company. Besides, it could be icy out there. I might slip and fall and break a hip."

She thought she was being charming, but the truth was, she did look frail. Certainly more than she had almost a year ago in April, which had been the last time he'd seen her. He held open the French doors for her so they could duck out onto the covered verandah, and he tucked her hand firmly into the crook of his elbow as they crossed the flagstones toward the smoking area. Only snow dusted the floor, not ice, but Marcia still clutched him tightly until they were on drier ground.

"Always a gentleman. No wonder your mother is so proud." She pulled a small cigarette case from her clutch bag and tucked it between her lips, which left a crimson smear on the filter. She eyed him while she dug in the bag for a lighter.

Her hands shook, so he steadied them with his so she could light up. The skin beneath his fingertips felt thin, like chiffon over porcelain. She must have seen something in his expression, because she laughed again, and this time, it sounded a little like breaking glass.

"I'm thin, I know. Not the good kind of thin. But what am I going to do? Everything tastes like shit, now. Except you, Joey. I bet you still taste like summer sunshine. Don't worry," she added with a long drag on the cigarette and a pause to let the smoke drift from her nostrils. "I'm not going to try to find out. Memories will have to do for me."

"I didn't know you were sick," he said in apology.

Marcia leaned against the stone railing of the balcony and shivered. Neither had put on coats before coming out here, and although the space was sheltered and featured several large space heaters, the wind swirled up now and then, colder than March was meant to be. She looked over the edge of the railing into the darkness below before giving Joe a steady gaze again.

"Nobody knows, really. Even the ones who should know are pretending they don't."

"My mother?"

Marcia's smile hung from one side of her mouth, crooked. "Your mom and I have been best friends since the fourth grade. We were each in each other's weddings. I was there when you were born, Joey. Literally there when the doctor pulled you out of her, because your dad had gone out into the hall when he couldn't deal with her screaming. No. Your mother doesn't know, and I'm not ready to tell her, yet."

At the end of that long-ago summer, Marcia had been the one to break it off between them. She'd divested him of his virginity with a matter-of-fact casualness, and still the way she'd ended things — abruptly and without excuse, just a simple "Goodbye, Joey. Forget to write" had lingered with him for a long time. Maybe still did. They'd never spoken of that summer again, and on the fewer and fewer occasions in which they'd found themselves together at family functions, Marcia had never once given so much as a wink or a nudge to bring up the subject

"Why are you telling me?" he asked.

"Because, sweetie," Marcia said, "I know for damn sure you know how to keep a secret."

She drew on the cigarette again, the tip of it flaring cherry red and orange until she stopped. She asked over the side of the railing, blew out a plume of smoke, and crushed the remains of the cigarette onto the stone.

"They should have an ashtray out here. Ah, well. Never mind. Someone will clean it up." She looked him over with bright eyes. "It's colder than a snowman's balls out here, but I'm not ready to go back in just yet. Put your arm around me, would you?"

He obliged. She leaned against him. He'd grown taller since that summer, and now her head fit neatly under his chin. Joe put both arms around her, keeping her close. She put a hand on the front of his shirt, inside his jacket, and curled her fingers around his tie to tug it.

"What happened with you and the blond princess?"

"She broke it off. I guess I wasn't husband material after all."

Marcia gave his tie an admonishing yank. "Nonsense. You're the epitome of husband material. Handsome. Successful. Great in the sack. So what did you do to ruin it?"

Everything about him went taut and tense. Marcia stepped back to give him a familiar sardonic smile. Joe swallowed the knife in his throat so he could answer.

"Because I ruin everything. Didn't you know that?"

Marcia's smile faded into softness and concern; he didn't like that any more than he'd liked her attempt at humor. "Who told you that? Never mind. I know. Well, it's not true."

"I didn't love her," he said abruptly.

"But you wanted to."

He nodded and turned to put his hands on the railing. "I wanted to. I tried to. I thought I could do it, Marcia. I thought I could be faithful to her, but in the end, I just...didn't want to be."

"Some men aren't cut out to play the part of faithful hound. But that isn't you," she added quickly when he looked at her. "You think it is, but it's not. So, you couldn't be that for Princess Priscilla. That doesn't mean you're not capable of it."

"Mom?"

They both turned at the sound of a lilting feminine voice. Joe kept his expression neutral, blank, except for the faintest hint of a polite smile. The woman who'd come out onto the balcony moved toward them, her arms crossed over her chest and her teeth chattering.

"It's freezing out here," she said. Her chin lifted and her gaze flared as she looked at Joe. "Hello, Joey. It's been a long time."

"Honey," he greeted Marcia's daughter with a nod. "Good to see you."

She cut her gaze from him. "Roger and I are leaving."

Honey and Marcia kissed cheeks and embraced quickly. Honey gave Joe another look. She seemed as though she might say something but in the end she only gave her mother a squeeze on her bare arm, turned on her heel and went back inside.

Silence. Marcia waited until the door had closed behind Honey before she turned to face him. Her mouth thinned.

"Oh my god. My daughter? You fucked my daughter?" She held up a hand to stop him from speaking and shook her head when he tried again. "No."

Joe didn't say anything else.

Marcia sighed.

After a moment, she shook her head again and took his hand. She squeezed it and linked the fingers through hers. She held it without saying anything for a long moment while he counted to five, then ten, inside his head, and then she let him go.

"Was it me? Am I the one who fucked you up?"

"No. Of course not."

She huffed out a puff of silver air. "See? You always were a good liar."

The words stung, but he didn't let it show. "I thought you said I always knew how to keep a secret."

"What's a secret," Marcia asked, "unless it's a lie?"

A small knot of partygoers burst onto the balcony, their loud laughter and the clang of them scraping the metal patio chairs along the flagstones to get them all beneath the heater. Marcia to a few steps away from Joe. Not blatant. Still obvious.

She caught his look. "I'm still a married woman, whether I like it or not, and I guess I'll stay that way until I die. No sense in giving anyone any ideas."

"No. I don't suppose there is," Joe said.

He helped her back inside, solicitous and making a small show of it; her loud gratitude wasn't meant for him, really, but for anyone who might be listening. Once inside the ballroom again, she let go of his arm and put some distance between them once more. It wasn't to keep anyone from thinking something was going on, but because of what she'd discovered about him and Honey. Joe didn't bother to explain that Honey had seduced him, that it had been hardly anything at all, that his memories of Marcia far superseded anything he'd ever done with her daughter. There was no excusing any of it away. He'd done it.

"Joseph. There you are. Marcia, lovey, where've you been?" His mother pulled her best friend into an embrace. Clearly, she'd been indulging in the champagne. Her cheeks were pink from it, her gaze flashing. When she looked him over, she didn't even have that lingering disappointment he'd grown so used to.

"Such a shame Priscilla couldn't be here tonight," Joe's mother said.

Oh, wait. No. *There* it was.

"That's what happens when you break up, Mom. I mean, there's still time. I could leave and you could give her a call. I'm sure she'd love to be here, too."

His mother frowned but fortunately seemed too tipsy to take offense. "It's just a shame, that's all. We all just loved her. Didn't we all just love her, Marcia?"

"We all just *loved* her," Marcia echoed, her gaze pinning his.

"I didn't love her," Joe said.

His mother blinked rapidly, then frowned. "Joseph. Don't be rude."

"I'm sorry, Mother. Of course. You look like you two could use some more champagne. Let me get you some."

His smile, the charm, the obsequiousness, worked. His mother's smile widened. She kissed his cheek, then patted it.

"There's my handsome gentleman," she said. "Marcia, isn't my Joseph just so handsome."

"Champagne," Marcia said. "Yes, please."

Dutifully, Joe got two more crystal flutes brimming with golden bubbles and pressed one into each woman's hand before excusing himself with a kiss to each of their cheeks. He didn't look to see if Marcia was watching him as he walked away; if she was, he didn't want to see the look on her face.

At the bar, he asked for another glass of wine. The bartender looked to be in her mid-twenties and wore her short brunette cut with a flair that matched her winged liner. She dimpled when he put a ten spot in the brandy snifter on the barter — an open bar wasn't an excuse not to tip.

"You look fun," Joe said.

She glanced around before answering, smart enough to make sure nobody was going to catch her flirting. "I can be. How about you?"

"I used to be," Joe said.

"What happened?"

He lifted his glass toward her. "I fell in love."

"Let me guess. It ended."

"It never started," Joe told her.

The bartender's finely arched brows rose. "Intriguing. You know, I generally find that red wine isn't the thing to drink for lost loves. That would be whiskey, my friend, and the hosts have provided a very good one, in my opinion. Care to take a shot?"

"Will you join me?"

She shook her head but gave him another of those lovely, dimpled grins. "Can't. Not until I get off work later."

"Will you then?"

"The body is willing, my heartbroken friend, but my own heart says 'no way.'"

"Sounds like you've had your own troubles with love." Joe took the shot she'd poured and pushed toward him. He lifted it. "Sláinte."

She rapped her knuckles on the bar and watched him toss back the shot. "Indeed."

"Would you recommend another?"

"I'm not supposed to encourage it," she said, "but as a side note, I do get a bonus from my boss for every bottle I make sure gets emptied tonight."

"And they're charged to the party bill?"

She grinned again but didn't speak.

The few glasses of red he'd been drinking all night hadn't warmed him nearly as much as the single shot of whiskey had done. The peaty, smoky taste of it lingered on his tongue and eased the slices left behind in his throat from his earlier conversation with Marcia. Joe leaned over the bar.

"How about you just give me the bottle, then. It's a win-win all around."

"Not for the party hosts," she said.

Joe smiled. "They're my parents. I think they can afford it."

"In that case, my friend, who am I to deny a man in need of a bottle's solace?" She twisted to pull a bottle of Bushmill's from the back bar. "Yours was the only shot I poured tonight. It's almost full. Don't go getting into trouble, now. Get someplace safe before you go drowning your sorrows."

"I promise," Joe told her. "You have a good night. And if you change your mind about sharing with me later..."

She waited, but his voice had trailed off. It had been natural enough to say he'd take her number. That he'd wait for her to get off work, and they could decimate this bottle together. They could help each other get over their lost loves together.

"No," she said softly when he didn't continue. "I'm not the one you need to talk to tonight."

"Who should I be talking to?"

The bartender wiped a cloth down the length of the bar, lifting his empty glass to get the wet spot beneath. She put the glass into a bin under the bar and pushed the whiskey bottle closer to his hand.

"Her. Whoever she is."

TWENTY-THREE

Joe knew better than to drive drunk. His head had been buzzing earlier, but although he had the bottle of whiskey on the seat beside him, he hadn't had any more to drink. Not until he got to Sadie's house, and there he got out of the car with the bottle in one fist, trying to convince himself not to knock on her door.

The rain had started a few hours before and now threatened ice. He turned his face up to the night sky, letting it pelt him. It stung like needles; he opened his mouth to let the frigid water fill his mouth as he shuddered. Faint blue-white lightning lit the sky above the rooftops, followed shortly after by the far-off rumble of thunder. The streetlights were a dim comfort he wanted to step out of, in case anyone was looking out into the street.

He unscrewed the bottle's cap and tried to take a drink, but his shaking hands spilled half the bottle's contents before he could get so much as a sip. He didn't need it, anyway, and didn't really want it, either. If he was going to do this — and yes, he was going to do this, there was no backing out now...he was going to do it as sober as he could.

With the bottle still in one hand, Joe took the steps to Sadie's front porch. There was a light on inside, so he knew she was home. He would think of a way to explain how he knew it was her house, how it wasn't creepy or weird that he'd looked up her address and driven past more than once already. She wouldn't believe him. He didn't believe it, himself. But he would tell her the truth. He'd known for months where she lived, but he'd been good enough to stay away.

He would tell her how he couldn't be good enough, anymore.

His knuckles rapped the door hard enough to sting. Whiskey sloshed in the bottle until he forcefully stilled his hand from shaking. He clenched his jaw to stop his teeth from chattering. He still wore the suit he'd had on for his parents' party, but he'd forgotten his coat.

"Joe?"

She stepped back, and he moved forward. Rain had slicked his hair over his forehead and now dripped off his nose. His clothes hung, sodden, the white shirt made sheer. He made a puddle on her rug and gave no greeting, no word of explanation, made no noise but the slightly raspy hiss of his breath.

He'd thought there would be words, but he had none. Only action. Joe put his arm around Sadie's waist and pulled her to him, hard, the bottle still in one hand and pressed now between her shoulder blades.

That kiss, that first one, crushed their mouths together hard enough to bring the taste of metal to his tongue. Joe kicked the door shut behind him without leaving Sadie's lips. She tasted like warmth and welcome, and if he'd had any doubts about her before, her open mouth and the gift of her tongue in his told him he'd made no mistake. At least not in this, not right now.

He moved her to the stairs, one, two, three steps, but got no further. He pressed her down and swallowed her gasp. The bottle slipped to the steps beside them.

"Sadie, Sadie, Sadie..." He couldn't stop himself from touching her everywhere.

Cupping her breasts, he slid the hem of her nightgown up over her thighs. She was bare beneath, and he touched her, over and over, every place he could reach, her skin satin-smooth under his fingertips. He pushed the gown higher as broke their embrace just long enough to look into her eyes. Sadie's gaze had bright and heated, the way she'd often looked when he told her those stories, and he took that as permission to bend his mouth to her breasts.

He'd sometimes been ashamed of imagining this, but there was no shame between them now. He took her nipples into his mouth, suckling each gently until she cried out and arched under his touch. All he could think about was tasting her. His cock, hard as iron, could wait. Right now he needed all of this to be for her.

She cried out, arching again when he put his face between her legs. Sweeter than honey, hotter than flames, her body welcomed his kiss and the stroke of his tongue along her tender folds. He wanted to devour her but kept himself steady. Concentrating. He found her clit with the flat of his tongue, licking until she gasped and lifted her hips, and then he lost it. Lips, teeth, tongue, hands — everything worked together as he traced the lines and curves of her body with his mouth. He'd lost the ability to be soft or tender, and there was no grace in this, how he went down on her, but her moans and cries and the way her cunt swelled and parted and dripped sweetness for him kept him going.

She looked down at him. He looked up, licking his lips. He swallowed, hard as thunder rumbled louder. He got up.

He'd been a madman to come here. To take her this way, without so much as a word. She lay on the stairs with her nightgown up around her throat, her legs and lips both parted. If he'd seen even the barest hint of an idea that Sadie didn't want him there, he would turn on his heel and run away. Run the way he always had.

Sadie drew in a breath, then another. She didn't move, not even to shield her body. She made no invitation with words, but with the look in her eyes and the way her body moved. Her breasts rose and fell with her rapid breathing. She bit her lower lip.

Haven't you ever done something just because it's easier to do it than not?

He'd said that to her once, on that park bench that had become theirs for all those months. Those words had been true then and they were also true now. Easier to stay here, yes, than to force himself to back up and walk out the door, but this was not about ease. He could no more have left her at this moment than he could have willingly stepped in front of a train without hesitation or fear.

Joe leaned in with a hand on the stair behind her head. The other went between her legs, his palm pressed to her flesh. He slanted his mouth to capture Sadie's again and kissed her slowly as his hand moved on her. She drew a breath and held it.

Neither of them moved.

Her breath slipped out of her on a low, shuddering sigh. Under his palm, her cunt throbbed, but he kept himself still. Slowly, slowly, and slowly, Sadie drew in another breath. Her breasts rose with it, tempting him to suckle her nipples again. He didn't move anything except his hand, pressing it to her.

No matter what he'd ever told her in the stories about his prowess, there was always, always a moment of uncertainty when he waited for a woman to come. Had he moved too much, or not enough? Had the moment been lost?

Looking into Sadie's eyes, Joe had no doubts about the pleasure overtaking her. She kept his gaze and held it as her body trembled against his touch. He could not look away from her; he would not, not even when the whiskey bottle as it got nudged from its place and fell down the final step to the floor below.

"Sadie." He found his voice. He put his forehead to hers. "Don't make me leave."

She had to be uncomfortable in this position. He slipped a hand between her body and the steps, hoping to ease any discomfort. She uncurled and stood, one step higher than him. She could look him directly in the eyes from this spot, and he waited for her to dismiss him.

His tie, already askew, came off with barely a tug. The tack at his collar foiled her for a moment, but Sadie didn't allow it to stop her.

She undid the rest of his buttons with swift and unfumbling fingers, then tossed his jacket to the floor. All the time they were kissing, kissing, and he lost himself again in the taste of her.

Sadie broke the kiss. Her gaze searched his once more as she took his hand. Stepping backwards up the stairs, she led him along the hallway as she helped him out of his clothes and pulled her nightgown off over her head. By the time we got to her bedroom, she was naked and Joe wore only a pair of damp boxer briefs.

He had asked her not to make him leave, but now, here, he discovered he could go no farther. All this time, Sadie had been the one woman he thought would never succumb to the shallowness of his charm, but he'd busted in here and used everything he had to get her into bed. He'd given her an orgasm. That didn't mean this was anything but emptiness, that didn't mean he wasn't simply preying on what he knew had to be her vulnerability.

"Joe," Sadie whispered, reaching to stroke his arm. "Come to bed with me. It's all right."

Still, he hesitated.

"Your favorite color is blue," she said. "You hate tomatoes and love cucumbers. You love a good red wine and sometimes drink whiskey, but you hardly ever get drunk. You smell like soap and water because you never wear cologne. I know you, Joe. It's all right. Come to bed with me."

He kept his feet, but his heart staggered and nearly sent him to his knees. For months, he'd imagined how he wanted her, but *want* and *need* were not the same thing. He needed her now. He had needed her since the first time he'd seen her there on the bench, although he hadn't known it or been able to admit it. He wasn't sure he could admit it now.

Sadie took his face in her hands and kissed him. She took his hand and pulled him to her bed, where she laid him down amidst the comfort of soft sheets. Under the blankets, she took off his briefs and tossed them out. Joe hadn't been aware that he was shivering until Sadie aligned her body with his to warm him.

Her fingers traced his collarbone and slope of his shoulders, her tough gentle but not light. It weighed him as she covered the planes and lines of his body with her palms. When she bent to taste his left nipple, he couldn't hold back the groan, or the gasp when her fingers trailed lower to grip his cock.

Joe had already learned that the taste of her was even better than he'd ever imagined, and now he discovered her touch was, too. He couldn't stop himself from pushing into her grip, his fingers threading into hair — not to force or even guide, but because he had to make sure this was really happening. No more imagination. All of this was real and true. He was no longer shivering.

Then, oh, yes, oh god, she took him into her mouth.

It lasted forever, that pleasure, as she kept him on the edge. He gave into every stroke of her tongue. Every caress. When she gasped and threw off the blankets, he pulled her upward to kiss her mouth. Their bodies once more fit together, every piece of them connected. His mouth on hers, her breasts crushed to his chest, the slick heat of her cunt against his thigh.

He couldn't wait any longer and rolled them, covering her body with his. Sadie arched and writhed beneath him. It would take only a single motion to be inside her, but he stopped himself. He had to stop. When she reached between their bodies to touch him, he buried his head in the curve of her neck and muttered a cry.

"Joe. I want you." Her whisper sent another rush of fierce heat to scald him, to light him up.

"I want you, Sadie...but..."

He was bare in her fist. She had to know, didn't she? Why he could not, would not ever take such a risk. She kissed him, pumping his cock in her fingers. His cock grew impossibly hard.

"Wait." He rasped the word. "Sadie, wait. Give me a second. Just...don't move."

"You mean, don't do this?" She closed her fingers, stroking.

Joe jerked, groaning, desperate and ready to spill even as he fought the sensation. "Ah, Sadie –"

She pulled him down, his cock against her belly and traced the line of his ear with her tongue. She urged him to pump his hips forward as sweat slicked their bodies. She hooked her ankles around the backs of his calves.

"I want to be inside you so bad," Joe said.

"I want that, too."

They moved together. He slid a thigh between hers, pressing upward with his cock against her belly, hoping this would work at least a little for her, because he wasn't going to be able to hold out much longer. Faster, moving faster. He moaned her name and found her soft skin with his teeth. He bit, too hard, he knew, but in this moment as they both writhed and groaned, it felt right. Her nails raked his back.

He came, breathless and dizzy with it. Hot slick warmth glued them together. Joe forced his lungs to expand, to take a breath, and he became aware of the slow rasp of Sadie's breathing matching his. He needed to move, so he didn't crush her, but he couldn't bring himself to totally relinquish the contact. He kept one leg thrown over her, his hand cupping her hip. He couldn't stop smiling.

He didn't want to leave the warmth of her bed, but when Sadie got up to go to the bathroom, Joe took the chance to tug on his pants and shirt. Shoeless, his clothes still wet from the rain, he braved the storm again to get to his car. He should've been smart enough to think of it the first time, but he wasn't going to let another chance escape him. He had condoms in the glove box, and it took him only a few minutes to grab a few in one fist and let himself back inside her house. He was back upstairs a minute or so after that, and he'd already shucked off his clothes so he could slide into bed next to her, naked. He pressed one foil package against her bare skin.

"Always prepared," he said against her throat.

Joe had always loved Sadie's laugh, and even more so now. He joined her. The bed rocked with the sound of their laughter, leaving them both breathless. It was as good as sex had been, this shared joy. She touched his face, her eyes wide. Mouth open. He kissed her.

Already, his body stirred with wanting her. But first, they talked. Everything they had become had been built with words, but now the ones he spoke were open and honest. Now, everything they said to each other was the truth.

Everything here was finally real.

TWENTY-FOUR

Joe awoke to the smell of pancakes, but he didn't go downstairs right away. Stretching in the sunlight shafting across Sadie's bed, he allowed himself to revel in the memories of the night before. He rolled onto his belly to press his face into her pillow, breathing in her scent.

It had really happened.

He showered quickly, wrapping a towel around his waist in lieu of putting on his damp clothes from the night before. Downstairs in the kitchen, he found Sadie at the stove. It seemed natural as anything to be there with her in the morning while she made breakfast, even more so to kiss the back of her neck. He slid his hands into the gap of her robe and found the weight of her breasts, heavy and glorious in his palms. Her nipples tightened under his touch, but after a moment he stopped and pulled away.

"This smells good," he said.

"Sit down. Help yourself."

Sadie had brewed coffee, and she poured them both mugs to sip while they ate. She didn't quite look away from him. She didn't quite look at him, either. Joe had woken with a growling belly. One hunger sated had left another roaring. Still, he put his fork down after a few bites.

At last she looked at him.

Making love to Sadie after so many long months of wanting her had been the culmination of dreams he'd tried hard to deny even having. He had learned so much about her, but sitting across from her in this early morning light, Joe could only hope he knew who she really was. He didn't want to ask but couldn't stop himself.

"Last night," he said quietly. "Are you sorry about it?"

"No. Are you?"

He shook his head. "No."

Never in any of his stories had there been a morning after.

"Do you want me to leave?" he asked suddenly, leaning forward to catch a glimpse of her eyes.

"Do you want to go?"

Her calm voice should have soothed him, but he'd heard that tone from her before. She spoke to him like he was a stranger again. It was his turn to look away.

"Joe," she said gently and waited until he looked at her before continuing. "I think it might be better if you did. I'm not ready for this to be anything more than what it was."

"What was it, Sadie? What should I do? Pretend it didn't happen?"

"Maybe that would be best."

"For who?"

"For both of us."

He got up, wishing he'd taken the time to pull on his clothes, even if they were still damp. "For you, maybe."

"Fine. Yes. For me. It would be best for me if you left." That calm voice again, putting distance between them.

If he could kiss her again, she might change her mind. Wildly, he moved around the table. If only she'd give him the chance — Sadie pushed her chair back with a screech of the legs on the floor. He withdrew, hating himself for scaring her but also for giving her any hint at all that he was bothered by any of this.

"Why?" he asked, finally, the only question he could find the words to ask.

"Because my husband just died, Joe, and I'm not in a good place to start anything new!"

"*This* isn't new."

She had to see that. She had to know. Yet so clearly, Sadie did not. She didn't feel the same about him as he did for her, and she never had.

She dismissed him, turning her back to put her plate in the dishwasher. "I'm sorry, Joe."

"You're not really asking me to go." One last try.

She went to the sink, keeping herself turned away. She spoke curtly, with a hint of anger. That was good. He wanted her to be angry, to feel something. Anything other than nothing.

"This is absurd," she said.

Joe tightened the towel at his waist, too aware that he was almost naked. "Why? Why is it absurd?"

"Because it is!"

"That's not an answer!"

Sadie turned. "I don't have a better one, okay? You can't possibly think we're ever going to be together. Because that's just messed up, Joe. That's really messed up. There are so many things wrong with that scenario, I can't even begin to list them."

"Try me."

She shook her head, once more turning her back to him. "No. No, I don't want —"

"Sadie." Joe put his arms around her from behind again. His chin fit just right into the curve of her shoulder. He breathed in the scent of her and closed his eyes. "I know you better than you think I do."

"I'm sorry, Joe. I can't do this with you. Not now."

"Because of your husband?"

At last, she turned in his embrace to meet his eyes. "No. Because of me."

He let her go and stepped away. He squared his shoulders. Let out a slow, long breath. He hid his despair with a firm voice and hands that didn't shake.

"Last night you said you wanted this. Whatever it is."

"How many stories have you told me?" Her voice was jagged and rasping.

"That doesn't matter."

"It does."

He frowned. "It shouldn't."

"I wish it didn't," Sadie said. "But it does. For years I've listened to your stories. Now, here I am, inside one. Right where I wanted to be all along. And I'm not sure what to do."

Joe sighed and put the heel of his hand to one eye, pressing against the sudden headache. Then he took it away to give her his full gaze. So tired of the stories, so weary of lies interwoven with truth, he said, "you are not just another story to me."

"I wish I could believe that." Sadie shuddered.

"But you can't."

"I'm sorry," she said.

"I don't want you to be sorry. Shit. Be anything but sorry." His hands opened and closed into fists at his sides. "What if we started over? What if we started at the beginning?"

Sadie spoke in a whisper. "I need time to make sure I know who I am. How can you say you know me, when I don't even know myself?"

"I wasn't the only one telling stories, Sadie. For two years I've seen you once a month, almost every month. I am not the only one who told stories. I just used more words, that's all."

They faced each other with a universe between them. He moved as though to touch her face but stopped an inch away, too afraid that the softness of her cheek would be the final undoing, that he would end up on his knees in front of her. Begging. He put his hand on her shoulder, instead, desperate for some contact with her.

"Why do you think I kept coming back, Sadie? Why do you think I kept telling you, month after month, everything about me that nobody else seemed to see?"

She looked steadily into his eyes. "I can't be your answer, Joe. I can't be the one who saves you from yourself. I don't have what you're looking for. I'm sorry, but I'm not ready to be your redemption."

Joe shattered, but slowly. The pieces of him stayed held together with his anger and disappointment the way a broken glass door will vein itself with jagged cracks but hold its shape until someone shuts it too hard.

She was still in the kitchen after he'd dressed and come back downstairs. Steam rose from the sink she hunched over. She didn't turn to look at him, even when he stepped through the doorway.

"From the first time you laughed with me, all those months, and all those stories," Joe said quietly. "They were all you, to me. All of them were you."

It was the closest to "I love you" that he could bring himself to say.

TWENTY-FIVE

In April, For the first month in over two years, Joe did not go to the bench on that first Friday.

He could not.

He didn't go in June.

He did not go in July.

He didn't forget about her. That would have been impossible. He just refused to allow himself to think about her.

There'd been a chance for the two of them, and he'd been willing to take it when she had not. There was nothing he could do to change that. All he could do was let her go.

THE SUMMER WAS MORE than half gone before Joe made it down to the beach. He liked being down there for the Fourth of July. The small-town parades and fireworks were always fun, even if the town was overcrowded with summer tourists. He spent a little over a week there before being pulled home.

Not for work. He'd taken vacation time, and although he hadn't shared anything about his personal life with the other members of the firm, he assumed that they assumed he was taking time to recover from the breakup with Priscilla. In truth, he did think of her a few times over the week, if only because he'd never brought her here. He'd never even told her that he owned a place in Delaware. He'd asked her to marry him yet had kept from her something so important to him.

He cut his trip short because his mother had texted him that Marcia was dying.

Marcia hadn't asked for him, but he still went. The four-hour drive home felt like twenty hours. He hadn't even changed his clothes and still wore the scent of sand and sea on him when he got to the house.

It took him a few minutes to steel himself to get out of the car. How many hours had he spent here? First, mowing the lawn. Then, making lazy summer-heat love in the pool house. And later, once, in the living room while he was on his knees, unable to get up, and Marcia had held and rocked him. The night that Eddie died.

Marcia Adams had been the first woman Joe had ever loved.

He braced himself to face Honey, but the woman who answered the door said that the family had gone out for a bit. Yes, he could see her. Yes, she was coherent.

"Oh, you," Marcia said when Joe knocked on her door. "Don't look at me. I haven't put on my lipstick."

Against the white pillows and blankets of her bed, she looked gaunt and wasted, but her smile was genuine. She let him take her hand. Their fingers linked. When he kissed the knuckles, Marcia let out a small sob.

"You're beautiful," Joe said.

"I'm not, but you've got that silver tongue. Your mother must have called you."

"Is it okay that I came?"

Marcia sighed. Her fingers twitched, but if she meant to squeeze his hand, she didn't have the strength. She closed her eyes and gave a faint nod. "Yes. It's okay that you came."

They sat in silence for a few minutes. Her breathing eased and slowed until he thought she might be asleep, but when he started to take his hand away, her eyes opened. Her lips parted, and she said his name.

"Yes," he replied.

She was quiet again. Her lashes fluttered, casting shadows on pale cheeks. She sighed again.

"You woke me up," she said.

"I'm sorry — "

"No," Marcia interrupted, her voice surprisingly strong. "I mean you woke me up, Joe. Back then. I never forgot you. I was forever grateful to you for it. I know I was abrupt when I ended it, but I thought it was for your own good. I wanted you to move on. It was best for you."

Again, he kissed her knuckles. He had words, but couldn't say them. His throat had closed too tight.

Marcia sighed. "You do not ruin things. I should have told you that then, and later, and as many times as it took so you understood that. Someone should have, and I wish it had been me."

"I was grateful to you, too. Not just for...you know," Joe said quietly. "For all of it. For giving me an expectation of what it could be like, with the right person."

Marcia gave another small, dry sob. "Promise me you'll let yourself find the right person."

"I thought I had. But she didn't feel the same way."

"Not the princess. Please tell me it wasn't her."

"No," he said. "It wasn't her."

Joe bent to press his face to the bed, shoulders shaking as he tried to hold back the flood of grief rising up inside him more forceful than any tide. Marcia let her hand rest on his head. She stroked his hair, murmuring words he didn't need to hear to understand. He got himself under control quickly, too aware that it would be awkward if anyone in the family came home. A visit from an old family friend was fine, but finding him weeping at her bedside would raise questions neither of them would want to answer.

"Listen to me. Don't give up. Promise me that, at least. Just...don't give up the way I did." Marcia sounded fierce, but tired. "Don't you settle, Joseph Wilder."

"I promise."

"Kiss me. Then go."

He kissed her.

"Now go," she repeated and closed her eyes again.

He made it all the way home and into his living room before he lost it again. The last time Joe remembered weeping was the night his brother died. Whatever sorrows had followed him since then had all been packed away. Now, everything came out of him at once. He went to his knees on the hardwood floor, not caring if he was making bruises. He cried for a long time, and when nothing more remained, he forced himself into the shower where he knelt again, letting hot water pound away at his back and neck until he thought he might be able to stand.

No matter how much he wanted to stay down, he *would* get up again.

He would not settle. He would not waste the rest of his life, and he wouldn't do this for Marcia. He wouldn't even do it for Sadie.

He would do it for himself.

TWENTY-SIX

August, finally

On the first Friday in August, Joe left his office at lunchtime. He stopped at his favorite sandwich shop. He went back to the bench in the park.

Sadie was already waiting.

This had begun one way and ended another, but one thing he knew for sure. Whatever it had been meant to become, he would do his best to honor that. Friendship, love, or if they were lucky, both together, making something perfect.

Joe sat next to Sadie. He looked down at his hands, linked in his lap. How did any new thing begin?

He straightened and turned. He held out his hand. Sadie took it.

"Hi." His fingers closed around hers. "My name's Joe Wilder."

"Hello, Joe," she said. "I'm Sadie."

Their fingers squeezed together. "It's nice to meet you, Sadie."

"It's nice to meet you, too, Joe."

Sitting in the sunshine with Sadie's hand in his, it was enough to be silent. To enjoy the touch of her hand. To drink in the sight of her smile, the one that did not falter or hesitate, the one that had always been so bright and special, just for him. Whatever mistakes he'd made could be overcome.

He had not ruined this or her or anything.

Sadie was the last story Joe would ever need to tell.

PLAYLIST

SHATTERED

I could write without music, but I'm so glad I don't have to. This is a partial playlist I used while writing Shattered.

SOMEONE YOU LOVED — Lewis Capaldi
    Best Part of Me (Feat. YEBBA) — Ed Sheehan
    Either You Love Me or You Don't — Plested
    Worst of You — Maisie Peters
    Wild Enough — Elina
    Skinny Love — Birdy
    July — Noah Cyrus
    What if I Never Get Over You — Lady Antebellum
    Let Me Down Slowly — Alec Benjamin

ABOUT THE AUTHOR

I was born and then I lived a while. Then I did some stuff and other things. Now, I mostly write books. Some of them use a lot of bad words, but most of the other words are okay.

If you liked this book, please tell everyone you love to buy it. If you hated it, please tell everyone you hate to buy it.

photo credit: Whitney Hart Photography

Find me here!
www.meganhart.com
readinbed@gmail.com

facebook.com/READINBED

twitter.com/Megan_Hart

instagram.com/readinbed

bookbub.com/authors/megan-hart

goodreads.com/Megan_Hart